MET BY MIDNIGHT

Star-Crossed Fairy Tales
Book One

Janeen Ippolito

Line editing and proofreading: Sarah McConahy
Formatting: Sarah Delena White
Cover Design: Yvonne Less of Art 4 Artists

This book is dedicated to Hope the Labradoodle, who faithfully sat next to me during edits (except when someone had a treat or said the "w-a-l-k word" or she got bored or someone delivered a package ;-))

Met By Midnight

Defiance is a whisper

In the darkening twilight before an undeserved death

Defiance is the clasp of hands

Before the final sacrifice

Defiance is the tear

On the cheek of a grieving daughter

Defiance is the choice

Of a dangerous mission into the unknown

Defiance is the surrender of will

Through an unlikely alliance

Met by midnight

For the greater good of a handful

Defiance is a whisper

Of love to the least

And this

And this

This is

Defiance

CHAPTER ONE

Her heart broke twice the day she found out her father was dying.

The first time was when Renna saw him carried off to the Room of Last Decay. The place where all Menders were taken when their bodies could no longer withstand the pain of recovering from Receiving. Only Attendants and Guardians were allowed to see them during the Last Decay, as their organs and marrow gave out, one by one, over-burdened by the inevitable weight of disintegration from too much healing. It was considered far too distressing to permit anyone else to view.

Before they parted ways in the reception chamber, she had clutched his withered, light brown hand desperately, only allowed a few moments for a final leavetaking. The silvery sheen to his skin, a sheen customary to Northerners, had faded to a sallow gray. A pile of fabric swaddled and cocooned his frail form.

What could she say that would have meaning? Eloquent words and a smooth cadence weren't her strengths. No, they had been her father's, Ertax Valtor, a priest of the Eternal in their small northern village. They had been her mother's as she sang, even while she was taken prisoner.

"No," Renna whispered. "They've taken everything else from me. They don't get to take you too."

He shook his head minutely, wincing with the action, as though he bore the weight of an anvil on his temples. "No. This is . . . as it must be." He inhaled a rattling breath. "Your mother Nephyna . . . myself . . . we only serve."

"And for what?" The Attendants looked her way. Renna forced a gentle smile, lowering her voice still further. "So they might take everything we have, everything we are, with no remorse? You said the Eternal was just. You served him faithfully. Where is the justice in this?"

"Justice brought us . . . here . . . according to the law..."

"The law seeks to use us, to squeeze us dry like water from a rag."

His cobalt eyes met her own, surprisingly firm despite the frailty everywhere else in his form. "Justice, like all things . . . comes with a price. For all. And it is a price we gladly paid, for you . . . to Receive..." He inhaled. "Maybe for you . . . to do . . . what we could not..."

A deep cough shook his shoulders, forcing him upright briefly. Renna could only rub his back through the thin infirmary garment, desperately searching her mind for what he meant.

All she found was empty space, regret, and the sharp, cold seeds of anger.

After that, he had laid back on the movable cot. The Attendants had urged her away, leaving her with the pieces that remained of her spirit.

Her heart had broken a second time when she was informed that same day of her own Pair Bonding. She had recently come of age at eighteen, and must be wed within a few months. She needed to meet her future spouse immediately.

Fury ripped through her. Of all the times! Could they not give her even a short period to grieve?

Still, they summoned her after taking her father away. The calm blue walls of the reception chamber drifted past her as she followed the Attendants. All those who passed through the Last Decay were permitted any comfort available to them. A cold reward for the merciless way their lives had been bled from them earlier. And if the Room of Last Decay was so merciful, why were they not permitted to see their own families? What else could the Sanctuary take from Menders?

Anger knotted in her stomach at the traitorous thought. Renna buried it deeply within her mind, as easily as she buried her hands within the oversized sleeves of her white robes and cowl. *No matter what, remain calm. Otherwise, they will see and know.* So had her parents warned countless times during her life. So had her mother's gray-blue gaze warned Renna before she had turned away.

Renna didn't understand what would happen if the Attendants knew the truth of her rebellious mind, her thoughts that wandered far beyond the Mender Sanctuary in the capital city of Syrus. Yet her mother's death soon after their gossamer captivity was enough caution that no matter what Renna endured, silence was the only recourse.

Still, she wondered why the Attendants had truly taken them away. Supposedly, for their own protection in alignment with the law of the kingdom. Menders, with their rare gifts of healing and aura reading, were too weak for life among others. Such a thing would crush them.

All lies. Ertax and Nephyna Valtor had not known any struggles. Her parents had Received when they were able and the need seemed great. Otherwise, Ertax had served as a priest to remote homes, and Nephyna had kept the household and spent her time clayshaping and weaving. Renna had only known peace in the northern reaches, and what friendships could be had in the local village.

Yet the Attendants still insisted that, as Menders, they could be taken advantage of by others. They were liable to be caught up in the dangers of living among the ungifted.

So it is important for the Mender Sanctuary to take advantage of us first. A grim smile teased her lips. At that moment, the nearest Attendant glanced at her. Fear tightened the knots in her stomach, and her lips straightened. Smooth as the plain, polished wooden walls of the hallways they walked through, passing by Rooms of Healing where Menders recovered from their latest Receivings and Courtyards of Serenity where they were meant to find solace among artfully groomed landscapes and splashing fountains.

Receiving. Solace. Recovery.

Never freedom.

Few Menders questioned this life. Many of them had been born into it, knowing little else. The Valtors had been among the last who remained outside. The Mender Sanctuary was safe, safe from the overwhelming presences of others, safe from the travails of daily life. Safe to atone for any sins, for some believed the gift of Mending was a curse from the Eternal himself, a punishment for past crimes.

Renna was different, and she knew better—or perhaps she knew just enough for it to chafe her soul like an ill-fitting shoe. She remembered having ill-fitting shoes, of refusing shoes entirely in order to run barefoot in the soil. Her feet were too big and too wide, nearly as large as her father's, although she was not nearly so tall. And truly, Renna simply despised excessive footwear. Running with the cool grass underfoot was far more ideal.

But that was before. Before the Sanctuary had smothered her in layers of fabric, of softness and deafness to the outside world. Including heavy shoes, stuffed with material that weighed her to the ground in a way both pleasant and unpleasant.

Although mostly unpleasant. Mostly in a way that made her want to incinerate every last part of the clunky, soft-soled horrors.

My Pair Bonding awaits. The thought drew her back to the present.

Her heart thudded as they made one final turn and stopped within the main Guardian Chamber. It was a circular room with curving wood that formed a dome, with everything painted in soothing shades of cream and pale gray. Candles flickered in plain metal holders on the walls. She had rarely met a Guardian, those who claimed supreme protector status over Menders. They had been given such authority and rights by the royal family of Searlen, Renna had been told.

A royal family who stooped so low to "protect" others from occupying their own homes was a royal family that had far too few responsibilities elsewhere. But as of yet, no one had ever asked Renna her opinion. Just as no one had questioned why her mother had died so soon after her supposed rescue to the Sanctuary. Just as no one had sought Renna's opinions about being Paired on the same day as her father's Last Decay.

Such ardent protection from my own values and opinions. At the thought, she could no longer suppress the lip twitch. Thank the Eternal, all attention was on another robed and cowled figure in the room. This one was taller than her, looming over her by a foot or more. On either side of him stood Guardians, recognizable only by their pale tan robes and cowls. They did not permit their faces to be seen.

What sort of protectors hid in the shadows? Yet even the usual defiant thought failed to comfort her. Renna swallowed hard, pressing her suddenly wet palms into the fabric of her sleeves.

"Corenne M'Valo, your time has come," intoned the Guardian to the right of the tall figure. "On the eve of the loss of one man, you begin your journey to know another, one who shall stand beside you for the rest of your days."

"Unless—"

The other Guardian's cowled head turned toward her. "Unless what, young Corenne M'Valo?"

Unless one of us perishes first, as my father is perishing. No, she mustn't say that. Caution, cool as water, still as ice.

Even though they still misspoke her name. She was Corenne Valtor, not the crude M'Valo with the prefix that reminded everyone of her existence as an action, not a person. As a Mender—M'Valo, of Mending—not an individual with a history in the northeastern lands of cold streams and thin, verdant trees and deep, narrow valleys.

I must be cool as the water after the first snowmelt.

For some reason, amusement filled her mind at the thought, as if someone, something, teased her for poetic thoughts.

Foolishness.

She shook her head. "Grief for my father has addled my words, Guardian. Accept my apologies."

"They are heard and accepted." With a slow nod, the Guardian turned to the looming figure. "Reveal yourself, Drius M'Lyra."

Huge hands emerged from his sleeves, pulling back his hood

to reveal a close-shaven head, deep-set eyes, and strongly carved features with skin the color of grayish-brown shale with a tint of ruby-rust. A Westerner, by his appearance—their skin matched the minerals from their soil, the way Northerners matched the silvery ore in their mountains. Not unattractive, but unknowable, as were all Menders, since they were immune to each other's power to read auras. As unknowable as the rest of her life, and equally out of her control.

Not him.

Drius studied her—or where he knew her face lurked beneath her own hood. "My sincerest regards."

A voice as stony as his skin. Perhaps she could grow to appreciate it, but would such effort even matter? She had no choice either way.

He's not the one.

The stirring filtered from the deepest parts of her soul, both utterly certain and entirely nebulous, dissipating a moment after it erupted within her. Not her words, yet as true as her own essence.

"And now you, Corenne M'Valo. Reveal yourself."

She did not hesitate. But yes, she did move in the slowest, most measured way allowed by the Sanctuary. At last her hood slid back, revealing the silvery cast to her olive skin, her dark hair, blue eyes, and round features.

At least she assumed they were as round as the rest of her had become, curved and soft. There were no mirrors in the Sanctuary to give insight into her overall shape or the contours of her face.

"My sincerest regards," she said quietly.

If Drius found her favorable to look upon, his gaze did not reveal it. Instead, he surveyed her with the same inscrutable attitude as ever. Renna supposed that was best. For there was nothing she could do to alter the current scenario. The Guardians had determined that she and the Westerner were the most suitable pairing for viable offspring, and that was all that mattered. Concepts such as compatible temperaments, passions, and even physical attraction were all unnecessary.

There was only one path for them: to Receive the pains and illnesses of others until the task overwhelmed their bodies and they were taken to the Room of Last Decay. The matter of Pair Bonding was to ensure that a suitable number of Menders remained for future generations and to garner any comfort companionship could yield. Comfort deemed necessary only because it would enable Menders to recover faster so they could Receive more injuries, more illnesses.

The Guardian to the right of Drius cleared their throat. "You are now revealed. In knowing each other's true faces, you begin the first stage of your Pair Bonding, and will pass through several more stages until all will be laid bare for the night of consummation."

Heat crept over her face. Renna had studied the book that indicated her duties for that night, but with the reality of it now before her, all she could imagine was running away. Far, far away with her robes tucked tightly around her.

Drius inclined his head in an answering bow. "I hear, understand, and accept."

The beginnings of the betrothal vow. Renna's face heated further as all eyes turned to her, awaiting her response in kind.

He is not of your soul.

She pressed her lips together. All of this, it was too soon. Far too soon for her, for her family.

The voice of reason, of pragmatism, at last took hold of her mind. It pressed back. *I have no choice.*

This wasn't right. She couldn't be here, couldn't be pledging her heart in this way to this person. All of this was wrong.

Agree, Renna. Keep your place to keep your life. Submit.

Her breathing shallowed. *I cannot.*

This wasn't fair. She understood the expectations upon turning eighteen, but her father was dying, her mother already dead. She had no one else. To give in now would be to lose the last piece of herself to a stranger.

Renna's word was her bond, as was the case of all citizens of Edrin. And now, to be sealed to a stranger, all because the Guardians mandated it?

Not to him. Never to him.

I cannot.

"Corenne M'Valo. Give your answer."

Stones! There was nothing for it.

So to her doom.

"I cannot." Her voice shook slightly over the final syllable. With a stiffening of her spine, she continued. "I humbly place myself on the mercy of the Guardians. The grief over my father is too near for me to consider vowing to become a Pair. Please, I beg of you, give me the span of seven days to make my peace. Then I will give my answer."

There was a swish of fabric and a rustling of voices as the Guardians moved away from the two Menders and sought each other's counsel. All throughout, Drius remained silent. Yet was that a flicker of faint relief in his stoic expression, or only the wishful thinking of her heart? She knew not if he were a kind man or a cruel one, but her words could be conveyed as dishonoring him, finding him unfit as a spouse.

Yet she could say nothing else. No other words.

This was wrong.

The light-voiced Guardian spoke. "This is highly irregular. Even for one of your upbringing."

"It is as you say. I was brought into the Sanctuary late in life." *And against my will, though even that I had to hide.* More words to swallow. "I beg your leave, but I am still not accustomed to such ways as yours. Even, perhaps, unfit for Pair Bonding."

The Guardians moved back to their former positions. The figure to the left of Drius spoke now. "Do you question the wisdom of the Guardians?"

Take care, Renna.

"No. I only freely acknowledge my own frailty and insufficiency as a spouse at a time such as this. You know I am adept at seeing and healing others, my leaders. Yet I fall short in estimating my own strength. It is in the greatest desire for truth of self that I reveal my own failings, though it may lose me the honor of a worthy spouse."

The words slipped from her as easily as water over stones in a streambed. Smooth and fluid, as though prepared. Maybe it was from the endless pressure of the Guardians and their edicts that her eloquence sprang forth.

Yes, that had to be it.

More swishing. More rustling of voices. More considerations, and more awkward moments of silence between Renna and Drius. Did she have a stomach at all? No, it was only an ever-growing, ever-tightening cluster of knots.

Eternal, let my words strike their mark well.

Let her have this one small freedom.

At last, all the tan-robed figures turned to face her.

"We accept your response," the light-voiced Guardian said. "At this time, your Pair Bonding will be delayed, and if another suitable Pairing is found for Drius M'Lyra, to her he will be given."

"I hear, understand, and accept." Renna bowed her head to conceal her relief as well as to show appropriate obeisance.

"So it is done."

Another figure spoke. "Your words are unorthodox, Corenne M'Valo, but we are satisfied by your willingness to speak truthfully of your shortcomings, even to your own hurt. This will not be forgotten."

"As you say, Guardian."

The underlying threat was as shielded as the robes they wore, yet clear as crystal to Renna. They would be watching her for signs of improvement. They might order her to additional precept meditations on the ways of the Sanctuary so that her mind might be tamed to suit. They might even increase her dosage of the mandatory morning and nightly herbal tonic meant to ease her addled, willful mind. And then, she would be Paired.

I cannot.

Even as the words echoed within her, Renna knew their truth. Her mother was dead. Her father lay dying from the relentless Mending the Sanctuary required to satisfy the odd need for penance and purification. Honor and sacrifice.

Sacrifice without voluntary surrender is not true sacrifice. It is coercion.

And she would have no more of it.

As Renna retreated into her hood and turned to follow the Guardians from the room, only one thought sank into her mind like a stone, anchoring in deep.

In seven days, I will be free.

It must be so.

Even if Renna knew not how or in what manner, still she and her father must be freed.

The time had come.
Something more awaited her.
It had to.
Even if it was only a dream.

He stares at her in silence
And nothingness
The winds of shadow and mist whirl around them
In a world beyond worlds
A time beyond times
He stares at her in silence
With shadows around them
She cannot know his form or face
Yet somehow she knows
He knows
Everything
Every falter
Every failure
Through it all
He will never
Leave

"I fought back today,"
She tells him, expecting
Anticipating
She will see that disbelieving smirk
Yes, there it is
Somehow, in the nothingness
Without sight
She senses it
In his mocking voice
"Did you now? Does a wordless star cry out?"

Familiar irritation fills her
Along with a longing as strong as spidersilk
"I fought back, with words. And won."
The shadows move, shift
As he learns what she knows
As she knows what he's learned
As hopes and fears and plans flow between them in a thousand ways

"Only seven days…"
"It will be enough."
It must be
It has to be
We must find each other
We must escape
"We must."
The words echo through the shadows
Before all evaporates
To dust and
Mundane dreams

CHAPTER TWO

He awoke with wetness on his cheeks and a hard, cold object pressed into his forehead.

A groan escaped him. Truly wondrous. He had fallen asleep on a book again.

Jaric rolled away from the tome and sat up, quickly taking in his surroundings. His private study in the royal palace quarters, with light wooden bookshelves built into every possible space, although not all were filled with books. Weaponry, curious objects, even empty spaces that only collected dust.

Humor sliced through him at the empty shelves. His sister Usilea often teased him, saying an empty shelf signified an empty mind. But if Jaric wanted shelves to stay unfilled, then they damn well would stay unfilled, because they were *his shelves*.

A swipe of his hand across his face and short beard revealed a sheen of water. The prince dared to taste it. Salty tears mixed with the faint odor of dog.

Something pawed at his rumpled pant leg.

"So, that was you?" Jaric glanced down into the face of a black-furred, medium-sized labordrim. A breed known for their webbed feet, superior sight, loyalty, and apparently, pleasure in licking their master's face when he fell asleep on the floor.

Opal blinked up at him, whined, and wagged her tail furiously. For some foolish reason, he'd allowed Usilea to name the dog, intending to change it later. But he'd forgotten, and the name had stuck. He scuffed his hands through her scruffy fur. "You need to be groomed again."

She bumped up against his hand agreeably, then backed up. He glanced at the carved brass timepiece on the wall. 10 a.m. Long past her breakfast hour.

His mind whirred. The late hour and the salt in his tears could only mean one thing.

Another dream.

He jumped to his feet and strode the few feet to his desk, flipping through his notebooks for the red leather one. The one that held the dreams.

Opal trailed behind him, quietly whiffling more complaints.

"One moment, Opie. Unless you want to find the kitchens yourself."

He grabbed a quill and ink pot, glaring at the book with its lines of numbers and charts of words and impressions. None of them amounted to much, but Jaric had to keep trying or he would be driven mad by what he couldn't control or understand.

When had he gone to sleep?

The pen scratched across the page, filling it with additional numbers and words.

He's dying. I can't lose him.

Unwanted, forced marriage.

I fought back.
Escape.
Find each other.
Leave here.

Jaric filled another page with vague images. Smoke trailing around long, thin trees and deep valleys. Deep blue eyes, soft with wonder yet wide with pain. A shiver of black hair, almost tangible.

"Tangible? None of this is tangible." He flung the pen down on the page, ink spattering across his desk. "I am losing my wits."

Opal leaped up, balancing her paws on his knee.

"What? Do you agree with me, then?"

She answered with a long, low series of woofs.

Jaric found a scrap of dried meat in one of his pockets and fed it to her. "There. Maybe now you'll be more useful."

She gulped down the treat and stared up at him expectantly. Fool. He hadn't even demanded a trained behavior from her. Then again, Opal did put up with what both Usilea and Keddyr called "Jaric's outstandingly odd moods." Naturally, they couldn't see the logical reasons for those moods in his mind.

He yawned as he stood up from the desk and stretched.

"Two years, Opal. Two years and nothing to show for it but a handful of notebooks." Jaric pulled down his dark blue tunic and walked over to the window. Through it, he beheld the vast, forested territory around Menirose Palace. Among those trees lay the capital city, Syrus. To the east, the various channels. Stretching out into the north and west and south, deeper crevices and mountains indicated they mined the minerals that were Edrin's main form of trade.

All of it he comprehended far better than the young woman who lingered within his dreams. No matter how vivid the nightly encounters, only a scant portion of them remained in the morning.

He was either mad, or she was real. And in danger.

She was *his*. Jaric clenched his hands into fists. They were joined, he and this mysterious woman. She might be enigmatic and impossible, but she was there. Above all else, he knew she was his to love, to protect, to care for as well as he could.

Claws scratched at his leg insistently. He glanced down and gave Opal a faint smile.

"Considering I can't even feed you regularly, some protector I would be."

She woofed and ran for the door.

He scrubbed his palms into his eyes, then made for the door. Enough dwelling for now. His own stomach demanded food as well, and then he had a sparring session with Keddyr. Perhaps that would clear his mind.

Just as he reached the doorway, a scar cutting down his arm caught his eye. Well, not just one scar. A number of small nicks and cuts and longer scars, for even at nineteen, he'd seen his fair share of combat skirmishes, mostly dissidents and rebels on the border. The royal prince was expected to lead some charges.

And my parents would have found it very convenient if I had perished while defending our lands. His lips twisted, matching the sour taste in his mouth. *A tragic loss, so young.*

And so very cursed, unable to be Mended. His parents loved him enough that he survived childhood. They were not as monstrous as that. Still, Jaric often wondered if, in their grand and showy visits to the temple of the Eternal, they secretly prayed for a quick, merciful death for him.

Far less worry for them, and after all, didn't that matter most?

He shoved the thoughts aside as he pulled on a faded black coat with sleeves that covered his wrists and a collar that concealed his neck. Sweat beaded his skin already, for the palace had only just been comfortable with his tunic. But now he wouldn't scandalize their Royal Highnesses or shock the populace with his unacceptable, unmended scars.

"And isn't that what matters most, Opie?"

The dog gave him a pleading glance.

"All right, you may have a point. I am a bit full of myself." He sighed. "Let's get breakfast."

An hour later, Opal rested by Usilea's side in the library. It was too much trouble to keep track of her in the midst of battle.

Jaric grimaced as he faced his opponent across the sparring ring. The other man was clad in the light armor of combat training, albeit without the usual tunic. Sweat streaked his deep brown skin, touched with garnet from the afternoon sun that beat on their shoulders.

And in opposition stood Jaric, clad in his tunic and heavy leather armor. The stalwart prince, eager to prove himself, challenging himself to endure difficult circumstances for the purposes of training. Or so everyone believed. His grimace deepened into a scowl. *If they only knew.*

He had no choice but to cover his scars.

His endurance was a punishment for the curse of his birth.

"At arms!" the herald commanded.

Jaric's gloved hand tightened on the grip of his sword. With one breath in, he acknowledged the sting of sweat on his brow, the weight of reinforced boots on his feet, the expectations of others on his mind.

Fight well. Always be better.

Don't get hurt.

At least, not any more than he already had.

One slow breath out. Releasing all warnings, all judgements. All physical discomforts of his unavoidable situation.

"Ready!"

There is only now.

And this time, Keddyr would not win. His friend could be incorrigible with that mocking grin and arrogant swagger. Even now, restless energy flooded through the other man, eager to be released through his blade. The aura of flickering fire, as it were. Enough to nearly burn Jaric.

Let him be fire. Despite the suffocating heat, despite his friend's overwhelming attitude, Jaric would be ice, outlasting any bravado or outrageous moves.

Be ice. No matter what they feel, it cannot touch you.

The words came from her, the mystery woman. They were true for all their ambiguity. As scattered as she was, her insight was honest.

"Lay on!"

At once, they began circling each other. Slowly. Oh, so slowly, especially on Jaric's part. He had no reason to rush and every reason to act as though snow flowed through his veins in lieu of blood.

A prettier metaphor than he was used to, but as before, it surfaced naturally within his mind, and it suited the situation.

Words are allowed to be pretty as well as useful.

Yes, she'd said that as well. If only he had a face to go with those words.

Keddyr leaped forward, teasing the edge of his blade along Jaric's. He pushed it aside with a flick of his wrist only to be turned back by a quick parry. But no counterattack.

Not yet.

His friend glared at him.

"Come now, Jaric. Show some sport!"

Stones, he could be irritating. Jaric rolled his eyes, pushing off the unrelenting heat again. "Giving in to your frantic testing is not a sport. Nor has it ever been."

"Aha, so you're still scared of approaching me. I see." Keddyr lunged in with another spew of quick taps at his blade. Always trying to set Jaric off-guard and go in for the kill. There was a reason Keddyr was known as the chief of swift bladework among the royal court.

Annoyance filled Jaric. It would be so easy to return Keddyr blow-for-blow and show him what superior strength could do against frivolous wind. Jaric's muscles clenched to do just that.

I won't. I will wait for the perfect moment, and I will strike.

The words were as calm as a cooling bath. Something he craved all the more as the bout continued, Keddyr still taunting, still testing.

The prince set his jaw.

I will wait.

All the more precious the victory, for the waiting. No matter what impatience he felt now.

He would wait.

Then he would match every blow. Effortlessly.

Keddyr's movements grew erratic, his panting heavy on the air. Despite his lighter clothing and stature, he tired sooner. He was far too used to quick tricks, and to them working as well. "Are you merely going to stand there all day, my friend? If I wanted to spar a wooden dummy, I would have purchased one."

Not yet.

Soon.

Very soon.

"You waste your breath on words." Jaric smirked, allowing one of Keddyr's feints to almost penetrate his defenses.

Almost. But it was enough to evoke a broad grin from Keddyr and elevate his confidence to just the right level. A confidence that Jaric could almost feel on his skin, underneath all the armor.

As ridiculous as that idea was.

"And you waste your time unmoving while others sneak in and steal victory."

With that, the other man feinted right, then left, pressing in close to ply his blade for the win, as close as possible to Jaric's neck without risking execution for treason.

Now.

Jaric lowered his blade and grabbed the handle of Keddyr's sword. With a sharp twist, he freed it from his hand and sent it clanging to the ground. With another swift stroke, he aimed his own blade at Keddyr's chest, right where his heart beat. Very loudly, it would seem, although Jaric wasn't quite close enough to detect it. He could only be imagining the beat.

Still, turning his friend's arrogance to fear added additional satisfaction to the victory. "There will be no stealing today."

"How did you last that long?" Keddyr fumed. "Blast it all, Jaric. You grow more and more steady and cunning by the month, no matter how I taunt. Who trains you?"

"Many people." Although truthfully, he had outgrown their teachings. This security came from somewhere else. Perhaps at the ripe age of nineteen he was finally learning to be at peace with the world. "And don't forget the testing of battle, which you have not had the privilege to experience."

Keddyr huffed. "I'm the heir of my family. They want me alive."

"Unlike mine."

"Jaric, I didn't mean it like that—"

"Don't bother denying what we both know is true."

The world would never be at peace with Jaric. But it didn't have to be. As long as his younger sister Usilea ascended the throne, Jaric's situation mattered little. Perhaps not at all.

He could disappear from the court and never be seen again.

That suited him for reasons both certain and uncertain. But always, ever wrapped up in the mysterious woman, for she would be coming with him.

Suddenly his feet flew out from under him, thanks to a sharp kick from his friend. The hard-packed ground of the sparring ring slammed into his back and he groaned, rolling to the side.

Oh, Keddyr wanted to play by those rules, did he?

"Aha, didn't see that one coming—"

With swipe of his left leg, Jaric sent his friend face-planting into the ground. Then the prince raised himself up on his palms.

"Beg pardon. Did I interrupt another fine pronouncement about your excellence and prowess?"

Keddyr spat dirt out of his mouth. "A truce! And then good beer and bread and meat."

"Agreed."

With a chuckle, Jaric moved to a crouch, then to his feet, offering a gloved hand to his friend. A handshake that turned into a rough hug with a slap on the back. Keddyr might be an ass at times, but he had proven faithful among the snaky nobility at court while still speaking truth to Jaric rather than endless flattery. Plus, though he was six years older, Keddyr never affected the attitude of languid maturity currently popular among the courtiers. Truly, there were many reasons Jaric did his best to avoid palace intrigues.

He'd be out of here soon enough, one way or another.

Nodding to dismiss the herald, they fell into step, exiting the forested training grounds through an ancient stone arch, and strode up the incline to the palace proper. The steep, twisted pathways through the forest were a fitting cooldown from sparring. The usual guards surrounded them, of course, although Jaric doubted anyone would be out for his blood. It wasn't nearly important enough.

Ahead of him, the brilliant red, yellow, blue, and white towers of Menirose Palace ascended in a riot of color and splendor. Crenellation was a contrasting color whenever possible, and every section that could be carved into a figure or relief sculpture, was—with gold and silver leaf atop it. He winced, rubbing his eyes at the cacophony. For a moment, Jaric was tempted to avail himself of his private entrance, but he glanced at Keddyr and dismissed the idea. He trusted his friend, but there was no need to reveal that particular secret as of yet.

In the end, it was there for her. No one else.

Thank the Eternal, the side entrance he and Keddyr availed themselves of was far plainer. The red door opened into white stone hallways with pillars on either side and dark green marble on the floor, rather than the ornate décor of the rest of the edifice. Even the torches were plain sconces on the walls. The crisp air trapped inside the building relieved Jaric's skin at last, even while his mouth ached for water.

He rubbed the back of his neck.

Keddyr's brown eyes surveyed Jaric carefully. "Might want to watch yourself there, your high-and-mighty-ness."

"What?" Yes, something stung to the right side, just below his ear. Jaric pushed aside his dark brown hair to feel the cut. "Not deep, and it's hidden. How did you see it?"

"I gave it to you, remember?"

"Yes, right before I bested you."

Jaric tried to keep the words light, but dread filled him. Another mark against him, quite literally.

Another stone-cursed opportunity for censure.

Keddyr clapped him on the shoulder. "You know I never tell if you don't."

"Agreed." He sighed, rolling out his shoulders, feeling the muscles release under his friend's reassurance. "Tomorrow, you have the usual visit to the Sanctuary?"

His friend nodded as they passed through another archway, avoiding as many servants as possible. "As always. You know the rules. Bodily fitness is next to godliness. And it is how we must serve the people—"

"—at our best. Yes." A ridiculous platitude for the nobility to feel better about using the Menders for even the smallest inconvenience. "The rules of court, are they not?"

"Unofficially, but true, my friend."

With that, Keddyr made his way down the hallway to the visitor's bathing chambers. Always keen to make sure he was fresh for any potential conquests.

Jaric paused in the hallway, frowning at nothing and fingering the cut on his neck. The blood had already clotted, and his hair would hide it sufficiently. Nevertheless, there would always be a scar. *An honor—and a danger,* he thought, considering his friend's unmarked form. The flawless skin and immaculate health of all the nobility and certainly the royal family, with Menders to Receive any and all of their hurts.

Except for him. The cursed prince. Unable to pass any injury or illness to a Mender. His bronze-garnet skin was more weathered than his friend's, marred with scars that could never be erased. Scars that could only be hidden beneath armor and clothing.

He shook his head. It wasn't that great of a crime to carry the memory of wounds. However, that thought was his alone against the nobles, the royal court, and most of the populace of Edrin. Even Keddyr and Usilea both believed that the use of Menders was as necessary now as it had been in the Channel Wars decades earlier.

Menders feel no pain. He reminded himself again of the rules. *It is their honor, their necessity, to serve. Else they would go mad from unmet desire.*

As usual, each word felt hollow within him. Wrong.

They were foul lies that entrapped Menders within the Sanctuary.

As usual, he focused on any truth beneath the feeling. There was no way he could know if the common beliefs about Menders were true or false. Jaric had never visited the Sanctuary. There was no need, and in any case, the royal family used a few select Menders kept in a separate location, so no one would know that the prince had never availed himself of their services. He could say nothing of their treatment. He could only mind his own.

Except for her. The young woman he met at night who wept as often as she smiled yet continued to Receive.

For her, with her, he had to find some way of escape.

But to do that, he had to *find her.*

He turned and lengthened his stride to reach his own rooms in the royal wing.

Opal would be awaiting him in the library, ready for her post-sparring rest by his feet as he read or studied. First he had to treat the cut before it worsened, and make sure it was hidden. Hopefully it would heal before the Royal Fellowship Ball in a few days.

After all, according to the outside world, the entire line of Searlen was free from fault or blemish. Their strength came not simply from their extensive mineral resources and placement near two major channels and the great Olsmark Sea, but from their indomitability of will and health. The well-being of all Edrin relied upon these beliefs.

Fools, all of them.

Yet Jaric would not be the one to unseat them. Not now. He had other matters to attend to, such as keeping his head down, ensuring he was left alone, and enjoying that beer and bread with Keddyr.

I will wait.

Somehow, he suspected his life would be upended soon enough. His parents had been quiet about him lately. Too quiet.

He opened his door.

Dangerously quiet.

She stares at him in longing
As if in all the world
There was none but him
A terrifying thrill
Tenses his—
Well, nothing
For they are formless here
Breathless
Yet never heartless
No, despite the shadows
He is more aware of his heart here
Than any other time in his life

"You are afraid."
Her words are sure and questioning at once
Yes, she knew that
Knew how afraid he was of losing
Everything
The fear was one of many aspects
That drew them together

"We cannot fail."
Was all that he could say
While wishing
He could only hold her close
For a single instant
Before all dissolved

Into shadows and memories
Of forgotten life

Chapter Three

Every morning, Renna awoke to the greeting of a small glass vial filled with brownish tonic. The Attendant never even spoke a word, only held out the container, barely larger than a thumb. With a sigh, Renna sat up from her bedcovers and drained every drop. As usual, it tasted like old leaves and dust. The Attendant gave a short nod within her hood and walked over to the next Mender, hidden by a wooden partition.

Wooden partitions, a dark gray curtain, a single box for the standard robes, and another box for personal items. That was all a Mender was permitted—or, as some Attendants said, a Mender was graciously allowed such things. It depended on whether the Attendant believed that Mending was a gift from the Eternal to be used at the exclusion of all else, or a curse from a past life that the Mender had to use to atone for their misdeeds. The second view was traditionally considered more unorthodox, but it had grown more popular over the years.

Her father's words echoed in her mind.

The kingdom now chooses to believe whatever will allow them to take without regard for the lives of others. It is the way of those who claim the Eternal's blessing yet walk in the shadows away from his light. Renna sighed. Ertax Valtor was right, but that didn't change her present situation.

At the very least, since the Attendant hadn't immediately summoned Renna to a Mending, she might have time in the music garden after consuming the breakfast that lay on the table beside her bed. Anticipation fueled her muscles, and she quickly chewed the hearty meal of rolls, meat, fruit, and soft vegetables. She pushed herself to the side of the bed and donned the layers of plain clothing, the dull white robe, and at the very last, the suffocating shoes. Thank the Eternal, her previous day's recovery from Receiving a bout of almswood pox had been swift.

With care that took every fiber of her being, Renna spoke to the Attendant and asked leave to go to the music garden, her favorite Courtyard of Serenity. There was a hesitation, followed by a short nod from the robed figure, then another Attendant had escorted Renna through the halls into the flowering oasis. Gardens were considered highly beneficial for healing, and thus, were another grace permitted to Menders.

She reached out to stroke a large purple bloom, ignoring the tsking from the Attendant on duty in the small space. The Courtyards of Serenity held gardens meant to be gazed upon, to inhale fragrant beauty, not to touch. Foolishness! Stroking the various blossoms and leaves could only be part of the enjoyment.

"Mender M'Valo, mind your actions." Neutral words, spoken by a neutral voice behind her.

Colorful language floated to the top of Renna's mind, but long years as the daughter of a priest had trained her to suppress it. Such words were unpleasing to the Eternal, and as much as she doubted his love at times, she had no other allies in the world.

Yes, I do. I have another ally.

More irrational thoughts. She pushed them aside as well.

"My apologies, Attendant."

"Noted and received."

Her insides twisted. The Attendant knew nothing of Receiving, of taking the pains of others. She set her jaw and walked quickly through the polished stone pathways until she reached the pinola. Ten polished mahogany keys interspersed with circles of amber, laid out over a wooden surface that stood at the height of her chest. It wasn't her favorite instrument, but the one that currently held her attention. Already her fingers were twitching, eager to explore the resonant potential within the instrument.

The music gardens were only a year old, a spontaneous gift from someone within the royal family. They had donated a number of instruments to the Mender Sanctuary. Renna couldn't imagine who this person could be, but then, she thought of the royals as little as possible.

Particularly at times like the present. Now, there was only the smooth, glasslike keys beneath her fingers, the spindly-sweet tones of the pinola. The soothing repetition of the simple tunes she knew, and the variations that flowed from her effortlessly.

"Mender M'Valo! You are called to Receive."

She blinked. Slowly, the sounds faded. "Am I, already?"

"It has been nearly two hours." The Attendant's voice was less neutral, more noticeably masculine in the rough edge. "And I have called your name five times."

Perhaps your voice was less compelling than the music. Renna gritted her teeth, choosing to release the irritation as well. It would serve no purpose and responding in kind might cause her to lose musical privileges or the clayshaping tools in her personal box. "My apologies, Attendant. I hear and obey."

Eternal, make me willing to do so.

As though her shoes were lead, she turned away from the pinola and left the garden at the side of the Attendant. Another series of hallways to the Receiving rooms, a final nod, and she entered the room alone. Well, alone except for the presence of the individual Renna was to heal. Someone all too familiar.

Seeing Lady Anlyn's face always gave Renna the urge to vomit.

The woman was kindly enough. An older widow of the court, halfway through her third decade, who kept herself healthy and well. A Receiver could not halt aging, only carry the burdens of disease, brokenness, and other physical symptoms. And honestly, Lady Anlyn was not yet old enough to carry more than the occasional wrinkle from too much laughter or a few errant strands of gray hair that disappeared under the onyx-dust cream she used.

Yet the noblewoman had one vice, and her breath stank of its residue in the healing chamber Renna had been assigned to that day. A peculiar mix of stale bread, rotten snow-peaches, and dried leaves that could only belong to her ladyship's favorite liquor. Likely indulged in after a very long night carousing while trying to seek a husband for the younger nobility she supposedly served as a matchmaker.

"Renna, my darling! Be a dear and draw those curtains for the sake of my strained eyes." She sagged against the carved white doorway while an Attendant closed the door behind her. "I must be made well. How else am I to share my latest exploits with the court?"

Renna gave a deep nod from the recesses of her hood. "As you say, my lady."

So it seems I do not have to speculate.

As usual, she felt the strange urge to meet someone else's gaze and share an amused glance.

As usual, she resisted the urge and it quickly dissipated into the remote reaches of her memory.

An absurd idea. Renna only met the eyes of others when she had to, as per the edicts of the Sanctuary. Eye contact was one step of the Receiving connection to non-Menders, as well as crucial component for reading auras. Her parents hadn't avoided eye contact with those they'd served in the northern reaches, so there must be a way around it. But naturally, the Sanctuary wasn't interested in a skill that would grant freedom to Menders. Attendants were always around. Always observing.

"Renna? Is there a problem?"

It should be Mender M'Valo, but Lady Anlyn never cared.

"No, no problem at all." Renna drew the curtains as the noble-woman requested, casting the interior of the room into dimness. There was little enough to illuminate, in any case. Two low white couches, well-cushioned, stood with their heads against the far wall and their lengths running parallel. The walls were a soothing cream, bordered with light wood and embossed with friezes of flowering vines and flowing streams along the top. A plain candelabra offered gentle illumination from the ceiling.

Nothing else was needed. No recovery tonics, for this was considered an easy Receiving. Renna stifled a grimace. If only she had not eaten so much at breakfast. As a Mender, her body would heal from the consequences of overindulgence far more quickly than Lady Anlyn's. Yet a small, wide-necked pot lay at the end of one couch for a reason.

Sometimes the Attendant would bring a recovery tonic as an

additional kindness. But considering how she had annoyed the last Attendant, Renna doubted there would be such care for her.

If she must, Renna would excuse Lady Anlyn from the room before expelling the misery of her guts. It would not be the first time. It likely would not be the last.

Would this truly be Renna's life?

No. It will not.

The origin of the certainty was unknown, but the strength of certainty was as solid as the tile floor beneath her soft-soled shoes. Her eyes drifted to the window for a moment, wishing she could see outside the thick, dark curtains.

Not knowing who she would be looking for.

Someone is there. Waiting.

"Well? Are you coming over here, Renna?" Lady Anlyn's quick, whimsical voice issued from the couch from whence she was already sprawled, her rich maroon and cobalt garments drifting around her, her rosy-onyx skin glistening with impatience and discomfort. "I have a grand new scheme to unveil to the court, if only my poor head and stomach would cease their grumbling!"

Renna swallowed a sigh, remembering the words of her father. *Always heal with caring, my daughter. Even through injustice, the answer is not to harm the ailing.*

Even if the ailments were their own fault.

She summoned words at last. "My apologies, my lady. Come, let me bear your burdens."

As the customary words slipped from her mouth, she settled across from Lady Anlyn. With a deep breath, Renna grounded her shod feet into the tile. With an exhale, she withdrew her hands from the overlarge sleeves, exposing her palms to the warm air, and extended them to the noblewoman.

More customary words. "Will you surrender your pain to one who carries it as feathers on their back, as a moment of shadow on a day of sunshine, as a single dissonant sound in life's symphony?"

"Yes, yes." Lady Anlyn flung her delicate hands out. "The sooner the better. This all grows so tiresome."

You aren't the one who might lose their guts in a pot. With a sigh, Renna suppressed the thought and took the woman's hands, lowering the mental walls that kept the woman's illness at bay and spoke the final words to focus her attention on Receiving. No matter the cost.

Then she met Lady Anlyn's eyes. Sparkling brown eyes threaded with willfulness and strength. With that gaze, she fell into the noblewoman's soul.

Tingles like pinpricks of hot needles flared on Renna's skin, each one latching on to a portion of Lady Anlyn's discomfort and pain, pulling it into Renna's flesh and bones, blood and marrow. As quick as lightning, as jolting as a stab to the gut, she Received every part of Lady Anlyn's complaint until there was nothing left.

"All has been Received. You are now Mended."

Nothing left but the throbbing in Renna's temples, the dryness in her mouth, the endless turning of her gut. She withdrew her hands, clenching them within her sleeves, and bowed her head, allowing everything she had felt and seen flow out of her, like streams over rocks. She pressed her lips together against the gorge rising in her throat. It wasn't proper to take medicine until the healed person had left the room. Some people felt terrible that Receiving harmed Menders—although rarely enough for them to stop going to a Mender if they could afford it or win the petition in court. Most enjoyed the delusion that Menders felt no pain.

"Much better! Excellent job as usual." Across from her, Lady

Anlyn clapped briskly. The sounds were thunderclaps in Renna's ears, now sensitive to all noise. "Just in time for the Royal Fellowship Ball in two days."

"I am pleased for you, my lady," Renna managed.

Speaking to the healed person wasn't required, but healed charges in good spirits reflected well of the Mender. With her recent refusal of a Pairing, Renna could use the additional favor. Even if each word made her head spin. She thought longingly of a particular elixir in the infirmary. It tasted of licorice and rosemary.

Can Lady Anlyn not leave already?

The noblewoman stood up, arranging her clothing with little flourishes and tossing her halo of curly black hair. "Indeed, hope comes every sunrise! Perhaps not for the prince, but for that friend of his, or perhaps the court accountant. Easy to gaze upon, and he does have deep pockets."

"I am sure."

Her head was surely going to explode. Somehow Renna imagined it would be easier to bear each Mending, but it never seemed to be so. Each time was a battle against the symptoms until they could be alleviated and full self-healing could take place.

Bile rose in her throat once more, pushing against every bit of willpower.

"Yes, well. I'm told you Menders have your own festivities and suchlike."

All lies.

Renna's hands trembled.

She wasn't going to make it.

"No."

Throwing back her hood—one violation of Mender edicts—Renna lunged for the pot and silently heaved up what remained of breakfast.

A second violation. The thought mocked her, even as she fought to maintain her silence. At least the Guardians didn't have to know of her failure. Unless Lady Anlyn told them, which given how garrulous she was, would be a likely outcome.

None of it mattered to Renna in that moment. Only expelling her insides.

"My . . . deepest . . . regrets—"

"There is no need, young one." The same delicate hands from earlier stroked her forehead, holding errant strands of dark hair back from her face. Soft cooing sounds echoed back to Renna's memories of her mother, the day Renna had caught a sickness from a visiting trade caravan.

Peace and guilt joined the twisting in her stomach. This could not be occurring. *She* was the Mender! No matter if it was fair or not, *she* was the one responsible for healing herself and others.

"I shouldn't have—"

"Shhh. Keep your voice down. I don't want you to get into trouble with those Attendants—which you will, won't you?"

Renna could only nod, lifting her chin from the pot at last. Tears coated her face. Lady Anlyn only clucked her tongue and wiped them away with the back of her inner sleeve, her face showing faint lines of disapproval.

"I knew Menders started young, but you cannot be more than twenty."

"Eighteen." What did it matter if she told anything more? She would already be in trouble for allowing Lady Anlyn this close. Besides, it was a great relief to share, a relief equal to the feeling of her empty stomach.

"Eighteen?" Lady Anlyn tsked. "You should be out trying to

catch the eye of a young man or abiding by your mother's side learning housecrafts or tradecrafts, not bearing the consequences of my late-night excursions. What a pity, to bear that level of wine-sickness without enjoying the wine!"

"As you say, my lady." Renna managed to lift herself up, with Lady Anlyn's assistance, to rest on her couch. "You should leave..."

"I'll wait until I see no Attendants nearby. And I promise you, they will never hear of this . . . incident. As far as they are concerned, you became violently ill after I left." She smirked. "A terrible way to leave a friend, but so be it."

"A friend?" Renna tilted her head, the word echoing within her in shock. Wonder. *Friend?*

"Yes, indeed. You seem as though you need one." She shook her head again. "I had no idea . . . although maybe that was the purpose of Menders keeping their hoods on."

Renna's throat tightened.

Should she dare reveal the truth? Each admission took her deeper into danger.

I'm already in danger every day I stay here, in a role that leads to an early grave.

But they had forced her into a vow of silence.

More coercion. I cannot maintain it.

Eternal, forgive me.

"It is," Renna admitted, her voice a sigh. "The hoods guard you from the truth of us."

"Hmph. Well, maybe I can request someone else next time."

Renna gave a slight laugh. "So they can endure the same pain?"

"Quite right, only . . . well, this is a mess, isn't it?" Lady Anlyn sat down on the couch across from her. "You know, I had a daughter. Lost her to a childhood fever when traveling abroad with my husband, where no Menders exist. They have other gifted." Her lips tightened. "After that, I vowed to keep myself from any pain . . . but she would be your age now, or nearly so. Not as round in figure, perhaps, although if she had taken after her father…" She clucked her tongue. "To commit yourself to this place so young, although I suppose you know no different."

Renna should only listen. She shouldn't speak.

But after so many years of silence, she couldn't help herself.

"I'm not . . . willingly here."

"What did you say?"

Renna swallowed hard. "My family lived in the north. The northeast."

"Yes, hence the silver touch to your skin."

"We lived at the edge of a small village. My parents Mended but also made things from clay and farmed. My father was the village priest. But when I was twelve the Attendants came. They brought us here, to the Guardians. To the Sanctuary."

The noblewoman raised spidery eyebrows. "Against your will?"

"As you say." The revelation left her as a huge weight from her chest, and an odd strength pushed her forward. "My mother died here. And now my father is dying after giving all to Mend others, for the Guardians tell us it is the only way to win surety in the afterlife. They gave him no choice." Before she could stop herself, she added, "I want us to leave. I want him to know freedom even as his life ends. Help us leave?"

The last words came out cracked and plaintive, the voice of a young girl who had watched her entire life disappear into folds of protective fabric and endless white rooms. Who had seen open fields and dreams of travel replaced with high fences around lavish gardens and days spent in bed healing from innumerable diseases and injuries not her own.

Who had been praised for her sacrificial gifts and her blessed calling, while knowing she had no other choice. Whatever hopes or aspirations she'd had, she would only be a Mender. Only exist for the sake of others.

Worthless unless she Mended.

It's not true.

But often, the words were hard to resist.

Renna realized Lady Anlyn had made no noise in quite a while. She glanced over, and her mouth dropped open. Tears streaked the noblewoman's painted face, and her brown eyes blazed with a fierce strength.

"Yes. I can help you leave."

"What . . . what did you say?" Renna paused. "I beg pardon, my lady, but—"

Lady Anlyn stood. "I am only a lesser lady of the court, unmarried and widowed, and as such, my powers are few. I cannot change the laws or enact new ones, and any ears I speak into will not aid you quickly enough. Indeed, especially since I do not know enough of your plight. But I can help you escape, if you are willing to help yourself."

Something in her measured tone awakened Renna's hope.

Eternal, could this be your answer?

"What must I do, Lady Anlyn?"

"Please, call me Anlyn." She leaned forward. "You must listen closely and do as I say. Be ready to leave two days hence."

Renna blinked. "To where?"

"You, my dear, are going to the Royal Fellowship Ball."

She could hardly breathe
Though that mattered little
In this place
Their space
Between life and death
Dreams and nightmares
She could hardly breathe
For she had hope
Streaming from her soul
Into his soul
Drawing them together
Through every meeting
Every night
Now
They finally
Had hope

"See me."
She asks.
"I cannot see you. Cannot know you. See me."

His anticipation
Is her only answer
But it is
Enough

Chapter Four

His parents were taking an everlasting time with this meeting.

For some unknowable reason, they continued to discuss the trade tariff dispute ad nauseum with the Royal Cabinet. Trade with other countries was always bogged down in technicalities, as his parents wanted to ensure their country maintained the tight borders they'd established after the Channel Wars. Every item had to be scrutinized, every travel document meticulously approved, every deal debated endlessly.

Especially deals involving Absteph, their chief enemy in the wars and still an uneasy neighbor across the Edrin Channel.

Still, the solution was simple. Renegotiate the terms so that citizens could purchase Absteph foodstuffs at lower prices during the high-mineral sleet rains in Edrin, and then raise the taxes on imported goods during the Edrin growing season. Allowing import taxes during the normal growing season would encourage purchasing from local farmers, and Edrin citizens who wanted to continue to import Abstephian goods were those of considerable means who would be able to pay the additional taxes. Any citizen who opposed the taxes could make their case at one of the monthly Court Petition Audiences.

Not that anyone in the narrow room would listen to Jaric, the first-born, yet without any standing in the court outside of his personal privileges as a member of the royal family. Each member of the Royal Cabinet sitting in the leather chairs around the polished wooden table was focused on protecting their own interests or pleasing his parents. For their part, King Obrik Searlen and Queen Giala Searlen presided over each end of the table as final authorities, allowing the debate to continue at their pleasure, heedless of the presence of their son and daughter in their corners of the room, supposedly observing as a form of political education.

Apparently, those lessons included how to expend vast amounts of time doing nothing while appearing to serve the people.

He tugged at his long, tailored coat and high collar, then shifted in his seat. A pity there were no windows in the room, nor even decent tapestries on the white marble walls. Ostensibly to keep the attention focused on the conversation.

All the better to increase the torture.

For some reason, the word "torture" spun in Jaric's mind for a moment, evoking a vague feeling of unease.

I know nothing of torture.

The words were of dream-origin, as true as the palace foundation beneath his boots. Menders were treated far worse than anyone else, or so claimed the young woman. Who might or might not be real.

She is real.

He sighed and leaned down to stroke Opal's head. The dog lay obediently at his feet, her expression equally bored and well-mannered. According to royal decree, no animals were permitted in high-level meetings. However, his parents had never protested Opal's presence, perhaps because they knew how to pick their battles.

Or perhaps they decided to throw him a bone to appease him, similar to how Jaric used dried meat to appease Opal. As long as he made no trouble for them, their majesties would tolerate him. He scowled and caught Usilea's eyes in the corner across from him.

His younger sister gave an answering grimace. Her deep brown face touched with garnet was a softer, narrower version of his strong, bronzed jaw and high cheekbones, but within her gentle features was a fearless spirit. As the crown princess, she would need every ounce of that fearlessness, especially at only sixteen.

Royal heirs in Edrin were chosen by the reigning monarchs. And Usilea had many reasons to carry the title. One reason they both preferred not to consider was her receptivity to being Mended, while Jaric remained insufficient in that area.

She would still be a worthy queen, even if that were not true.

Later, he would tell her his ideas about the trade tariffs, which had still not been resolved. Usilea might be able to move their parents where Jaric could not. She was cleverer in that way.

He inclined his head to her slightly and she smiled ruefully, acknowledging the salute to her fortitude. As well as the acknowledgement of her fear and the tightness in her stomach.

Well, he assumed it was there. Jaric had no proof of such an inkling. Only a vague sensation of her complaints as he met her eyes, as absurd as that seemed. How could he have any idea of her complaints?

He gave Opal's head another scratch, then sat up and turned his attention back to the meeting.

Queen Giala cleared her throat, her bronze face a mask of authority, her dark hair in a tight twist. The sapphire tint to her skin deepened. "And now, we turn to the matter of the Royal Fellowship Ball, including the special political situation of this year's celebration."

Jaric straightened in his chair.

"What special political situation?" he mouthed to Usilea.

She only shook her head, her golden eyes bewildered.

"Indeed," King Obrik replied, a slow smile on his powerful features. "It is time for Prince Jaricob to finally choose a suitable bride."

The words were heavy stones in Jaric's ears. *Not this again...*

He had a bride. Possibly.

In his dreams.

Yes, because that is certainly something I can tell the court without accusations that I've lost my mind.

"He will announce his bride the night of the Royal Fellowship Ball, in front of everyone, at midnight. There will be a grand betrothal celebration following the proclamation. After the wedding, Prince Jaricob and his new bride will be granted the title of the Duke and Duchess of Motarn and sent to manage the far northeastern province."

Everyone around the table, dukes and duchesses, court accountant and master of ceremonies, all gave murmurs of agreement. Irritation prickled the back of his neck. How wonderful to realize the entire royal court was content with his essential exile. Although the king and queen held power so tightly within their own schemes and unknown intrigues that the Royal Cabinet was wise enough to curry favor when possible.

None of that knowledge erased the truth of his dismissal.

This is not an evil.

Jaric had always preferred to be around fewer people, and the northeastern provinces, with their colder temperatures and rugged landscapes, were quite an acceptable exchange for the confines of palace life. There was only the matter of the bride.

She would love the northeastern province.

But the royal family would despise a Mender out of their proper place. At least, his parents would.

He felt Queen Giala's gaze upon him. "I trust you have a woman in mind, Prince Jaricob?"

"You know, Queen Mother, I have been so consumed with other responsibilities that it seems I haven't been able to decide." Not that the women of the court had ceased their pursuit of him, even Lady Anlyn, who had outlived two husbands.

His heart belonged to another, even though she might not exist. No, she existed. She must exist.

See me. See me.

He just hadn't met her yet. The statement was stone-hard fact.

I will know her when I see her.

In the span of his thought process, King Obrik had walked over to Jaric's chair. Now his father loomed over him, his orange eyes narrowed. "You will find a suitable bride by that night."

His tone allowed for no defiance—and at that moment, Jaric was of no mind to defy. It made little sense to protest. Instead, he needed to discover a way to escape the ball and find the mysterious young woman.

That would be a far more worthy endeavor. His parents had not left Menders out of the realm of possibility, likely because they knew Jaric would never meet a Mender.

They were wrong. He would use that to his advantage.

"Agreed, King Father." He raised the side of his hand from forehead to heart to nose in a salute. "As you have spoken."

Surprise flared on King Obrik's brown face, along with a hint of warmth and relief. But he only returned the salute and turned back to the main table, giving the same salute to Queen Giala.

As one, the monarchs spoke.

"And now, this meeting of the Royal Cabinet is adjourned. May the Eternal shine on our decisions this day."

A pronouncement as elegant as it was pointless. His parents only honored the Eternal when it suited their purposes. At least Jaric's doubts and questions were honest.

I want to believe. But I don't understand.

Surrender was far harder than it looked, especially when he already had so little power.

The king and queen exited first, followed by the Royal Cabinet members, leaving Usilea and Jaric to bring up the rear, a tradition of those who were and would be the greatest becoming the least. But his parents never had to remind Jaric that he was the least.

At last, he rose.

"Heel, Opal."

The labordrim leaped up and looked at him quizzically.

This again? "Heel."

She only blinked innocently. Little minx knew what she was doing.

He nudged his hand to his pocket where more dried meat lingered, much to the distress of the royal launderers. "Heel."

The dog's dark brown eyes lit up, and she obediently fell into step at his side. Finally. Why he kept the furry nuisance around was beyond him.

I need someone who will appreciate my intelligence—or at least my intelligent dispersal of treats.

Jaric walked over to Usilea, offering her his arm.

"Ready, my Princess Sister?"

She swatted his arm. "No more of such formal speech. Not when you must explain why you were so at ease with their ultimatum."

"I have found a certain contentment with my station in life," he said dryly, placing his hand over hers.

They walked through the arched entryway into the hallway beyond. More white marble, covered with intricate tapestries of Edrin's history interspersed with torches in bronze sconces. Silver and gold threads highlighted the ascension of the first monarch seven hundred years earlier, followed by centuries of peace—and then the Channel Wars, where three other countries attacked Edrin, desiring its ample mineral resources and central location. It was only the rise of the Menders that enabled the Edrin military to win. When King Rialt, the first of the Searlen line, had come to power, he had vowed that the Menders would never again be overlooked for their healing gift, and that they would be honored for their vital role in society.

Is captivity honor?

It was said that Menders preferred their Sanctuary in Syrus, that they found no greater meaning than in using their power. But somehow Jaric knew that to be wrong, or at least dangerously reductive—not that he was ever permitted to speak with a Mender. Usilea had little to say of her experiences, other than the Menders seemed caring, but aloof.

More questions he would have to answer.

She squeezed his arm. "Come now, out of your thoughts! Answer me. Do you have a woman you would choose as a bride—and who would choose you in return?"

A smile curved his lips. *I might know of someone.*

"I must have such a woman, or else I wouldn't have agreed to this situation."

"That is not an answer, Jaric." Usilea made a face. "Which means you have no one."

"I did not say that."

Hopefully, he had someone.

"Then what do you say?"

He shrugged, scratching at his short beard. "I say, Lea, that the matter will be resolved the night of the Royal Fellowship Ball."

"For someone so direct, you can be so cryptic. It's as if you don't care that this shapes your future for decades." She gave an elaborate sigh and glanced down at Opal, now heeling at her side. "What shall we do with him, Opie?"

The dog tilted her head to the side, then trotted over to Usilea, nudging her skirt for a treat.

"Traitor," Jaric grumbled, then continued. "I suspect we'll enjoy what little time we have left before I leave for the northeastern province." He gave his sister a more serious stare. "And you must endure our parents alone."

Sadness stole the teasing from Usilea's face. "Trust me, I am aware. For this, I fear the most." Her lips trembled in uncharacteristic fear. "Sometimes I wonder, Jaric, with all that I am learning of how this country runs, whether I am fit for the role."

Her terror teased at the edges of his senses. He yearned to ask after her fear, to help her speak through her doubts. But from the moment of her appointment as heir, Usilea had been privy to matters he could never know. Jaric would not threaten her honor by asking her to betray those secrets, even though he suspected some of them.

She had enough worries—that was all too clear. He could not be much, but he would be her ally for this moment, even without knowing what ailed her so.

Pulling her close, Jaric gave her a quick hug. "You are fit. And you will make this kingdom even greater than our parents have."

"I will try. For so long, I have tried. I am trying to make my own plans." For a moment, her face seemed far older and more cunning than he had ever seen. Then she sighed and was once more his younger sister. "Thank you."

They parted and continued onward. Usilea's brow furrowed. "This is not the way to my quarters, or yours."

"No, it is the way to the kitchen." Jaric winked. "What better way to ease royal tension than with tea cakes and chocolate and roast game?"

She grinned. "And seasoned ground-leaves with pepper-rise!"

"Yes, you rabbit."

"You have no reason to talk, wolf! Would you prefer your meat raw, then?"

"Only sometimes. It lets me share it with the dog." He flicked the edge of her nose, allowing the levity of the moment to carry his worries away. "And be careful who you mock, for I have some strategies about the trade tariffs and other economic matters that our parents are mishandling."

Usilea raised her eyebrows. "Always certain they are being mishandled?"

"No. I'm only certain when I'm right."

"Well, maintain that assurance at the upcoming ball when you choose a bride."

He rolled his eyes, but her words sank in nonetheless.

The Royal Fellowship Ball would indeed solve the problem, one way or another.

He only hoped the right woman was there. That *she* was there.

And that he would know her when he saw her.

He could hardly bear
The weight of waiting
For her touch
Her presence
Beyond insubstantial vapors
Of resilience and tears
Bright curiosity
Quiet observations
Like and unlike him
Close to him
Yet never cloying
Or controlling
From her, he felt
More of the same weight

"Where is your customary patience?"
He teased, to ease her worry

She met his words with fear
"I have much to lose."

"We have," he corrected.

"…we…"
Wonderment filtered through shadows

"We. Always we."

A pause
A space for fear within him

Then, a quiet reassurance
"Yes. We."

Always
We

CHAPTER FIVE

She had to make it. She had to.

Renna's feet pounded the pavement, the thick slippers of a Mender offering little relief to her aching heels and toes. For one who spent the majority of her time in bed healing from illnesses and injuries, such exertion was both exhilarating and exhausting.

Largely exhausting on the whole.

But she had to keep going, hated shoes notwithstanding. Her feet were too wide and flat—too large, overall—to fit any shoes Anlyn possessed.

Why she must wear shoes, Renna still had no idea. But she must, and they must be covered with fur as per the most recent fashion and in order to hide them from any suspicion.

She must still avoid suspicion. That had not changed.

This was her only chance. According to Anlyn, the Royal Fellowship Ball made the palace entrances as porous as cheesecloth, the goodwill of a royal family grown fat and slothful, without fear of harm. After all, they had Menders like her to seal up their wounds and carry their burdens.

No more. At least, not for Renna and her father. If they could only escape the Sanctuary, they would be free. No longer slaves, ever healing the hurts of others. They would experience life for themselves and earn their own wounds. They would be restored to how life was before their captivity.

If she could only make it through the dusk-shadows and down the manicured pathway to the carriage ahead of her. It was the last one headed for the palace grounds, free of charge to anyone who wanted to go and had bought their admission or procured a ticket from the public lottery.

She clutched the ticket tighter. It had been given to her by Anlyn, who had surrendered it easily, declaring she could host her own private party on such a night. It was for that reason she claimed need of a Mender within her home for the night, as she suffered from untold ailments of a sudden nature, and it would be a shame to waste the party. It was an unheard-of luxury, granted only to the very sick—and also to someone of Anlyn's means, so she said. She had even managed to dismiss the need of an Attendant to watch over Renna as she performed her supposed healing duties.

But only for part of the night. By midnight, Renna must return to Anlyn's estate, ascend the gravel driveway and narrow hill she now descended alone. For Anlyn could not be seen with her in the light of day. The woman was adamant that she should have as little public association with Renna as possible.

"Money and manipulation can do many things, Renna dear," she had said. "But even I know my limits, as little as I like admitting them, and they are regrettably many. As I said—you must help yourself and mind yourself. I will assist you with the rest of your needs once you return."

Renna had twisted her long white gloves in her hands. "What of my father?"

The noblewoman's lips had thinned. "I am doing my best to see to him as well. Trust me in this. I will see you to safety. Perhaps that will be some atonement to the Eternal and honor the memory of my daughter."

Then she had advised Renna to put on the gloves, which reached halfway up her round arms, just over her elbows. They were tight on her arms—where Anlyn was tall and willowy, Renna was shorter and square and curved—but she managed to get them on. Thankfully, they were in fashion. Renna already felt exposed enough without her customary robes, with so much of her skin revealed.

Sweat slicked that skin now, and locks of curly dark hair flew around her face. Renna released the ticket into the reticule at her waist. One of many foreign items she wore, all thanks to Anlyn's oddly curious generosity.

Hold up the skirt hem to avoid muck. The remembered words from Anlyn compelled Renna's hands. She held up the deep blue skirts that flared in a wide bell, the warm summer breezes toying with the delicate sleeves capping each shoulder with a thread of lace. It was one of Anlyn's finest dresses, but apparently not a favorite of hers.

A part of Renna longed for the simple cotton layers worn by Menders, but another part relished the chance to try something new and delighted in the silky feeling over her skin. Even though the corset pushed at her lungs and constrained her breath, the security of it provided a certain comfort and support.

The carriage driver, clad in the finest gold-and-red livery with silver-toned olive skin like hers, waved his hand, only ten paces ahead of her. His polished blue carriage stood in the center of all the great houses in this part of Syrus. "Last call for the final night of the festival! Any ticketed guests are welcome to attend the Royal Fellowship Ball!"

"I'm coming!"

The driver glanced her way and narrowed his eyes. "And you are, Miss?"

"An attendee." Renna slowed to a more decorous pace, pressing a hand to her chest. A chest that had been powdered and was more visible than she was used to. Anlyn had insisted the neckline was actually quite tame for the current styles, and that Renna was simply shaped in a way that "gave men something more to look at, though it wasn't quite the fashion, and other girls your age would be consuming fewer meals to compensate."

The idea was incomprehensible. She ate what was given to her to stay healthy and fit, to heal from the injuries and diseases of others. And yes, she did a few more exercises than others, but her muscles longed for the activity. She had been a child born of the cold mountains and broad fields of the homestead, not of confinement and delicacy. Even if a simple run now winded her.

Thank the Eternal, her attitude would apparently not expose her.

Act any way you wish, Anlyn had said. *They won't expect a certain standard of behavior because all are invited, including peasants, if they win the lottery. Your Mender quirks will not be noticed as long as you remain calm and keep your attitude light. Do look at others fleetingly, but do not gaze at others as though you seek their faults.*

Ah yes, the Mender's gaze. Well, fortunately Renna had learned to disguise that early enough. But now she must avoid Mender stoicism as well.

She gave her best attempt at a giggle.

"I was so occupied with preparations that I didn't notice the time," she added, automatically matching his Izven accent and speech cadence. Adept mimicry, made possible through perceiving someone's aura. Another quality of the Menders, used to set their charges at ease. Everything was done to make sure ordinary humans never considered that Menders had no choice in the healing, just as Anlyn had been fooled until Renna had given herself away with ill-timed vomiting. But her stomach had given her no choice.

Menders had no choice in anything. Not even when they died.

My father is dying from the incessant Mending.

Renna bit her tongue to force down the anger, making a show of fishing through her reticule for the ticket.

He nodded, relaxing at her tone and at the appearance of her ticket. "I see. Well, please take a seat, Miss...?"

"Ria," she supplied. Similar enough to Renna so she wouldn't easily forget. Hopefully. "Ria of Gheren."

It was the name of the nearest village to her parents' former homestead. Near enough to Izven to account for her accent, but not so near that the driver would ask after her. Eternal willing.

She stepped up into the carriage, easing around the other occupants and trying to settle her skirts, as per Anlyn's instructions.

Recognition spread across his burnt silver features. "Aye, that makes sense. Glad to have someone from the northeast here."

The northeast.

The cold streams, the high mountains. Her heart ached.

"Yes, although I've lived in the south for much of my life."

"Well now, who wouldn't?" He chortled. "A lot finer down here—and there's the Mender Sanctuary for any serious ailments, or not so serious, if you have the coin."

Menders living in a cage. No way out.

She gave her best effort at friendly smiles to the few others in the carriage, then stared out the window. As Anlyn had predicted, one of the men gazed over her figure once, and then once again. A pleased warmth flowed through Renna at the attention, but it cooled quickly into dread. She didn't want to be noticed and hoped to avoid any further attention as the carriage made its way over cobblestone roads rimmed with thick, well-groomed brush and vines.

Were other Menders content within their cages? Content with short lives in beds of healing, wrapped in bandages and coated with salves? Those who only knew the Sanctuary had been trained to be so, according to Renna's own experience. They were trained to be submissive. To be obedient. To never think of themselves or for themselves except in the snatches of time they had to study Guardian-approved texts.

The ache deepened within Renna. If the Eternal had truly made everyone for a unique purpose and reason, then that had to include the Menders. Menders were the same as everyone else—the same variety of eye colors, builds, and skin tones befitting Syrus. The only element that set them apart was the healing gift. A blessing and a curse, the recent martyrdom texts declared. Anyone born with the Mender ability must have been cursed in a past life, and so redeemed their life in this one by the unremittent healing of others.

The carriage turned and began ascending the long, winding road up through dense forest to the palace. Her stomach fell to her back at the hairpin curves. Her mind followed suit as she pushed away the lies of the Guardians and remembered the truth. According to her parents, those recent texts were not written by the Eternal's prophets, but were of later analysis, interpretations by those favorable to warfare and a decadent lifestyle without the consequences of injury. Whether or not someone believed the martyrdom interpretations should be their own conscious choice, not mandated by those in power. Just as the healing of others should be voluntary.

Beliefs her parents had imparted to her at a young age. Beliefs her father Ertax had proclaimed as the village priest of the Eternal. But that had not stopped her parents from being captured. Or prevented her mother's death. It had not stopped Renna from coming into her gift at the Sanctuary, or from being assigned her first charges, or from being introduced to her first Pairing.

Yes, she had evaded that fate, at least for the moment. But the underlying threat of the Guardians was real. She would be matched to another within a month, perhaps two, at the most. She would be given a few years of childbearing. A few years' reprieve from healing to ensure the next generation of Menders was safely born. Then she and her spouse would Receive more and more charges. And far too soon, Renna would face the same doom that was killing her father.

Not if I can do anything about it.

The strength of the words came from deep within. From a place of assurance, beyond reason or hope.

She didn't know how to fight. She didn't know how to reason in the courts.

But she knew how to mimic. She knew how to blend in.

She was not giving up.

There were places, Anlyn had said, where people of less repute crafted fake papers for a fee. Including precious, rare travel papers. The countries of Pomura and Absteph didn't have Menders. She and her father could disappear within the populace. But travel to other countries was extremely limited, and all travel papers had to be stamped with the seal of the royal house of Searlen.

Renna set her jaw. Stealing was forbidden in even the most ancient texts, but she wouldn't be stealing. She would be tracking down the royal seal and pressing it into wax, making a perfect copy of it, finer than any other the black market had. No one had ever broken into the royal chambers successfully—that was the pride of the royal household. Though their public areas were open, it was not so with their personal quarters. Anyone who entered a royal chamber was family, either through blood, marriage, or special trusted privilege.

Yet she had to break in. She had to copy the seal.

Anlyn had said that the people of less repute would accept such a useful gift in exchange for falsified travel papers for Renna and her father. Perhaps they would even help them escape.

She wouldn't steal, she would only copy. Just as she Received— in essence, copied—the illnesses and injuries of others. Her only skill.

Not stealing. Bartering.

It was a slender argument, a slender justification.

A slender hope.

But it was all Renna had—even if she had to push aside her qualm over falsifying papers.

A raucous laugh interrupted her musings. Two of the other passengers clapped each other on the shoulders and grinned, apparently having become warmly acquainted in the half-hour journey. Renna tilted her head. How could they be so comfortable when they had nothing to offer each other? No exchange of services? It was foreign to Renna after life in the Sanctuary.

Why had Anlyn assisted Renna? Ah, Renna knew too little about such things! She remembered having friends before being taken captive. So much earlier. But among Menders, strong relations were discouraged. They were never given time alone, and even in monitored rest were kept separate from each other. All the better to allow them respite, the Guardians said.

Renna had never quite believed them. Never understood how being around others could harm her or others. More secrets.

More mysteries.

More lies.

The carriage jerked to a halt on the cobblestones. She glanced out the window and gasped. Broad gardens rimmed by flowering hedges covered the grounds, lit with innumerable candles flickering in ornate lampposts. And through the window on the other side of the carriage rose an immense palace of brilliant yellow, vibrant blue, and fiery red, framed with towers topped with pale blue turrets. Menirose Palace.

Her mouth dropped open. Neither the cloistered life of the Sanctuary nor her free childhood in the wilds of the north had prepared her for such beauty. Such colors. Such life, as exhibited by the numerous people who filled the palace's courtyards and terraced paths.

Did she dare to walk in?

"Here we are!" announced the driver. "Last carriage of the night."

You are meant to be here. At this time, at this place.

She didn't quite understand the origin of the thought, but she would embrace it. Especially considering her purpose here.

Renna could ponder magnificent palaces and mysterious lies later.

Right now, she had to save her father. Her only family.

CHAPTER SIX

Eternal, someone save him from his family.

"You must choose someone tonight, Jaric." His father looked him over, his eyes narrowing. He adjusted the ornate golden crown on his head. "You must understand your responsibility. Do you?"

Jaric suppressed a sigh. "Yes, my King Father."

That earned him a sharper look, for the royal line had never required such honorifics among family in private conversation. But the old man could hardly fault him for excessive respect, could he?

For that was certainly what it was. Respect. How could it be anything else, like disdain? No, Jaric was hardly ever disdainful. Certainly not.

"Jaricob Searlen the Tenth, mind your tone." His father's words were deceptively gentle, even as he leaned forward in the throne in the private royal alcove, set apart from the rest of the ballroom. The throne was an elegantly carved relic from time past. If his family could have used Menders to preserve it, they would have. As it stood, a special team of servants dusted, polished, and oiled the carved wooden edifice every day.

His parents were another story. They had both benefited from the use of Menders since they were children, and their faces were unlined and pristine though they were over sixty years apiece. The results of nary an illness, perfect constitutions, and immediate healing from any ills.

I have more wear than they. It was a thought that brought him a grim, perverse comfort. Though it was always a reminder that he could not be Mended. That he was a blight upon the royal lineage.

Although truly, his parents' apparent longevity was notable—and enviable—to others in the court.

"Your injuries cannot be Mended." His mother echoed his thoughts, leaning forward, her thick, rich black hair framing her angular face, held back only by the golden circlet on her head. "And since you must serve our country despite your malfunction, you must have children who will not carry your affliction."

"And how do you know they will not?"

The king harrumphed. "We do not, which is why your sister was chosen as heir." Usilea shifted slightly, uncomfortable in her throne. "But as the prince, you are still under scrutiny. It becomes more and more difficult to hide your unsightly appearance. See to that mark on your wrist at once."

"Oh, so you noticed that?" Jaric grinned, picking at the cuffs of his long white sleeves until they covered the offensive pale line of a cut, still healing from yesterday's adventure carving in the woodshop. It was an activity unsuitable for a prince, but stones! What else was he supposed to do in the palace and grounds? Besides choose a bride, which lacked challenge. He would know her when he saw her, and he had not seen her yet, otherwise he would have chosen her, and she him.

See me.

I will, he thought back, as if she could hear him. His notes from their last nightly encounter had been even more vague than usual. All he could remember was that something had changed for the mysterious woman. Something of great significance.

"And I may choose from *any* at the Royal Fellowship Ball tonight, peasant or noble or merchant. Yes?"

His parents exchanged a pained look, then his mother nodded. "Yes. Provided she is suitable and exceptionally reactive to the healing touch of Menders, we care not her class."

"And choosing from the merchant or peasant classes might be politically astute," King Obrik added. "Your sister's betrothal secured peace with Absteph, and yours might well curry favor with the lower classes. A clever idea."

A smirk cut across Jaric's face. "Yes, I am capable of those once in a while."

He shifted his shoulders in the tight constraints of his black coat. No matter how the pressure of the heavy fabric centered him, he still wished it gone because he didn't have a choice in the wearing of it, which instantly relegated the garment to hateful.

Not that he would protest here. It was wiser to pick battles carefully—and, well, there was a long ball to return to and abandon. Jaric needed to reserve his strength.

For at the end of the night, he would leave this place. He would choose a bride who was a Mender, disguise her traits enough for them to marry shortly after, then be sent away to maintain the obscure dukedom apart from the rest of his family. His new wife could finally return to her homeland.

Or, they would flee the country. That was an option as well.

He sighed at the same time as his sister Usilea. To her credit, her lips quirked in a bit of a smile. The perfect crown princess, inside and out, but at least she had a sense of humor.

She rose from her own throne in the private alcove, settling her gown around her. Her brown skin, touched with garnet, gleamed against the yellow sleeves that rested just off her shoulders. "Come now, brother. Let us leave this tiresome conversation to the elders and see about finding you a wife."

"Yes, indeed. As always, focused on important matters." He briefly bowed to their parents, then offered Usilea his arm as they rejoined the Royal Fellowship Ball.

The usual mixture of nobility, merchants, and peasants mingled in the large hall especially created for summertide festivities. The pale gold walls were cut through with designs to allow pleasant breezes to circulate. Considering the palace was perched on a steep hill with layers of interior walls, if the guests were allowed to this point by the guards, they were deemed safe.

Jaric scanned the room with his usual disinterest. He had long suspected a marriage of convenience would be his lot. His parents had hinted as much so he could prepare to make the appropriate match from among his friends, or at least have a marriage of mutual connection. Despite their vain proclivities, the king and queen did care for him in their own way.

But instead, the advance notice, the looming doom of matrimony, had only made him more skeptical. Particularly as he became acquainted with the woman in his dreams.

Look. See her.

The command was as true as a promise.

A sharp elbow to his ribs caused Jaric to look at Usilea. She smiled teasingly.

"You're thinking too much again, brother of mine." Her voice was barely above a whisper, and her smile never faltered as they walked among the guests, spreading kind words and the usual alms, all to further the love and respect of the people. His sister enjoyed such occasions in short intervals, and even Jaric did not mind them too much.

"Is not the choosing of a spouse worth much consideration?" He paused to exchange pleasantries—and the usual few coins of festival-gift—with a man in a threadbare suit coat and frayed ascot. Once past, Jaric continued, "Your own betrothal took years of negotiations."

"All while I was a child, which was also the only time I have ever met him." She rolled her eyes. "All thanks to Mother and Father's insistence on tight borders and keeping me close."

"Yet weren't there paintings?"

"Yes, which may have benefited from the artist's brush to ensure Prince Cowan appears favorable. Furthermore, you know Abstephians. Their skin changes color with their moods. How can an artist capture that?" She shook her head. "I will never know his true form until we meet two years hence. Nor his voice. I've sent letters, but he doesn't reply often, and his words are stilted."

"Perhaps his family censors him." Jaric knew enough about that.

"Yes, perhaps. Or perhaps he is dull and formal and stilted." Her brow wrinkled. "At least you are permitted to choose."

The usual traces of melancholy filled her tone. He squeezed her hand. "Our parents and I will never allow Prince Cowan to mistreat you. You will be well."

"Yes, but will I be happy?" That slight pitch to her head, a slight quiver in her usually firm mouth.

He shook his head. "You know that personal happiness isn't the true end of politics. It has never been. Not for either of us."

"I know." She set her jaw, her face returning to its usual placid expression. "And I will do my duty as sovereign. Always."

"I know, Lea." Jaric gave her a faint smile.

Usilea would be an admirable ruler and was entirely committed to her royal role. It would never do to say that he envied her. Still, at least she had some sense of purpose and focus in her life outside of siring children and staying out of the public eye.

Not that Jaric desired the public eye, but ultimately, he did wish for a choice. Any choice. Which was why he was determined to find her.

See me.

She knew him, as he knew her. Even with all the mystery, this Mender would be a far better choice of a bride than someone who would be thrilled at his attention and care little for anything of substance beyond that. Nobility wanted political affiliations, merchants wanted status increase, and peasants? Well, there was a reason he had kept his attention on them more.

She is a peasant, or was one.

Perhaps she would want to teach him something, cause him to amend his desultory ways, if she could find any. Keddyr was far more capable of being disreputable than Jaric. Jaric just wore the demeanor more appropriately.

He searched the crowd for the shaven head of his friend, finding no one. A frown touched his lips, then vanished. Ah yes, Keddyr had taken up Lady Anlyn on one of her private parties at last. No good would come of that, Jaric was sure. But it was not his fate to decide.

"What about her?" Usilea tilted her chin toward a woman dressed in a secondhand gown of faded red, who ate copiously from the dessert table as though she hadn't seen food before. Judging by her bony figure, maybe she hadn't.

A pang hit Jaric's heart. She was not his woman, but she obviously was in need. "Perhaps, although I'd hate to distract her from a good meal."

"True." Usilea paused in consideration. "Shall I ensure that she and her family receive more than one such indulgent feast?"

He gave a quick nod. "And see if permanent improvements can be made to the surrounding village to increase their situation."

"Funds taken from your account?"

"Take what is necessary. I trust you."

She sighed. "I'm not certain I trust *you* in this. Brother, if you keep spending your inheritance so frivolously, there will not be much left."

"I can't take it with me, Lea." He shrugged. "Unlike you or our parents, if I'm injured, there is only so much a traditional healer can do. Every moment should count in some way. Gold in the coffers means little compared to that." He smirked. "Besides, unlike you, I have learned some methods of earning income—"

His foot twisted sideways on a suddenly slick surface. Jaric darted a glance down. A puddle of shining blue silk from the train of a dress. Most women knew to pin up their trains at the festival—and the peasants couldn't afford trains.

The thoughts flitted through his mind as he struggled for balance, jaw clenched with the effort. A head injury would take weeks to heal in isolation.

Always in isolation. As though others might catch his immunity to the Menders.

Solid, olive-toned arms with a faint sheen of silver caught him. A northerner. A breath sucked in somewhere above him where deep blue eyes widened, framed by short lashes and a narrow nose that some would have considered overlong. They would have been wrong. Her nose was perfect.

"Your . . . Highness?" The words were spoken with a quiet enunciation, as if the speaker were tasting each one to make sure it was a good choice.

Odd. Like everything else, from the bluish veins threading around her eyes to the thin curve of her lips. Nothing adorned her face, and there were other northerners at the ball, yet she seemed different, unlike anyone else. Luminous in the way of a cracked and broken diamond, gleaming facets with sharp edges.

Everything about her was perfect, even her imperfections. The scar across her eyebrow, the way her mouth quirked to one side. The way her gloved fingertips reached out, oh-so-carefully, to stroke his hair—

Her. It was her.

Another face invaded his vision, the complexion far warmer and more saturated. Usilea's expression was pinched in worry.

Stones! Why did they have to be in the middle of a crowded ballroom?

"Jaric?" She shook her head. "You can't be seen like this."

"I agree," spoke the diamond woman. His beautiful, frustrating mystery. She gave a quick, light trickle of laughter. "Have I not told you to remain steady and cool as snow?"

Had she?

Yes.

He remembered those words. He remembered her, though they had only met in dreams.

With her assistance, he was deftly eased back to his feet. Along the way, his muscles remembered they were quite strong and able. Hopefully his mind would catch up as well.

As he set himself to rights, his sister tugged down his left sleeve, which had been pushed up over his elbow, exposing a row of scars. Ah yes, that was what Lea had meant. No one could see him like that.

No matter. He needed to speak to the mysterious woman.

Except the woman, the Mender—had vanished. He scanned the room, heartbeat speeding up. Where had she gone?

He had to see her again. He was meant to see her again. Fear twisted his heart. Did she not recognize him? Maybe she did, with the line about being cool as snow, but she was being coy. Was he meant to initiate their conversation? Stones, why?

A tugging at his arm directed his attention back to Usilea, her face still creased in concern. "Jaric, are you sure you are well?"

"I cannot become ill from being caught in a fall, no more than anyone else," he muttered. "I may not be able to be Mended as you are, sister, but I'm no more prone to injuries or illnesses."

She blinked at his tone but shrugged it aside with a slight raise of her eyebrows. "Who was that woman? I've seen many mismanage their skirts, but she is by far the worst. Perhaps instead of alms, a greater kindness would be a lesson in decorum and manners."

As a Mender, she would never have managed a skirt before. At least, he could assume she had not.

"What, so she can use it at her spinning wheel or mucking out animal stalls? Be reasonable." Jaric sighed irritably. In all the warm room, heavy with conversation and fragrant smells, there was no sight of the young woman. Curiouser and curiouser.

Why had she left?

He suddenly spied a flutter of deep blue silk sliding over the appreciable curves of his cryptic rescuer. She stood at the far doorway. The one reserved for the royal family and nobility. As he stared, the woman tucked a long strand of dark brown hair behind her ear, smiled at the guards, and began speaking to them.

What was she doing? Was she trying to find him?

What else was the mysterious dream-woman doing here, if not to meet him?

He untangled his arm from Usilea's.

"Where are you going?" she asked. "Has someone caught your eye after all, my fickle brother?"

"Yes."

As though there could be any other answer.

He made his way across the crowded room as quickly as he could without arousing attention. He wanted to be the one who confronted her.

To hold her, at last.

He reached the guards just in time to hear one of them sigh.

"I'm sorry, Miss. There are no doing favors, not for anyone." He caught a glimpse of Jaric and stuck his chin out self-consciously. "Now go on and enjoy the rest of the party."

She gave another small smile, strangely similar to the guard's own, as if she were mirroring him. Jaric tilted his head. Her stance also matched the guard's, and when she spoke, her words followed the same cadence and accent.

"Are you certain? It will only be a moment. I mean no harm to the royal family and will disturb no one." Her voice lowered. "Please, it is a matter of life and death."

At that, the guard wavered.

I fought back with words. So she had said once.

Had she? Where?

"Well..." Disbelief tightened Jaric's stomach. The guard, Gerit, had never been tempted once by a pretty face or a desperate plea.

Yet this quietly daring woman with her intense stare held him in uncertainty. Where were the other guards?

Jaric scanned the room. Felos was at the fruit table, nibbling a strand of orange bemos-berries. And Ishin stood nearby, her gaze out of focus. He shook his head, unsure of whether to accost the mysterious woman himself or observe her and see how far she could go to achieve her goal, perhaps even understand the source of her power. The way she mimicked the guard was similar to the way he mirrored Keddyr's actions in sparring.

What gift was this? Certainly not associated with Mending.

At least her tricks hadn't affected Jaric. He paused, remembering the unsettling feeling after she'd caught him, as though his entire world had shifted as much as his physical stance. Well, she'd not affected him in a way that had removed all reason. Although reason had never seemed to enter his nightly encounters with her.

A moment later, Gerit stepped aside, allowing the woman to slip in behind him. And that damn train caught in the door after her. Jaric shook his head, bemused despite himself. An oddly powerful little ghost, but also oddly naïve. With a nod to Gerit—who looked quite baffled and more than a little fearful at failing his duties—Jaric followed the compelling blue dress through the hallway. There were more guards at every corner and doorway, of course, but maybe she could cloud their wits as well, if that was even necessary. These guards were trained to assume that anyone in this section had been expressly allowed in, unless there was reason to believe otherwise.

What sort of sorcery was this? And why did she believe it was a matter of life and death? Yes, her father was dying, or so he had written down in his dream book. But why come here?

Does a wordless star cry out?

But her actions . . . those were another matter entirely. Why would the mysterious woman be sneaking into the palace and ignoring him? Yes, she had a place in his heart, but there was still much he didn't know about her. Much that he didn't remember.

Better to shadow her steps to see if her actions betrayed her intentions.

Before the end of the night, he would learn the truth.

CHAPTER SEVEN

If I act as though I'm meant to be here, I will appear so, and none will question me.

She silently repeated the words, her mind whirring ceaselessly as she made her way through the halls of polished white stone. Periodically, gilded frames signified new doorways of richly carved dark wood. Somewhere among these doorways was the key to Renna's freedom and happiness.

Although, if that were true, why did it feel as though she had left every chance of happiness behind her, in the forest-green eyes of Prince Jaricob Searlen? A man she had just met, yet somehow, had known forever, if her heart was any indicator.

Renna paused in her movements, letting out a long, slow sigh.

He had seen her. Stared at her in a way no one had. As though she alone were the most precious creature in all the lands. Both distrusting her and trusting her completely. She raised a hand to her forehead, rubbing the tension there. A quiet groan escaped her lips. All of this was too much. She was only here to get the royal seal.

Wasn't she?

Almost unconsciously, she found herself turning around, reaching out a hand as if to return to the ballroom. To seek out the prince and dare to ask questions.

No, it was more likely if she sought him out, she would find her mind blank of words to speak. Or else she'd speak too many words.

I don't have time to think of this now! She smacked her hand against the wall. *I am here for my father. For our freedom.*

With steps that felt even heavier, as though her shoes were laden with lead, Renna turned and began her search again. She tested one doorway. Locked. Another. Also locked.

Footsteps sounded. *Someone is coming!*

She raised her head and faced forward, matching the servant's manner and stride, tripping on the hem of her dress only after they had passed. Renna tweaked the corset, trying to give herself more room to breathe as she searched.

Of course, there is always the prospect that I won't find the seal at all.

As before, the thought pinched her heart with fear. She clenched her fists to stem the shaking, then released them, tapping along the wall to steady her nerves. Tap-tap, tap-tap—skip over a wall sconce—tap-tap. The Menders had many methods of bearing with fear, since it so often occurred in their lives, along with pain. And as she had been taught, Renna faced the fear within her mind.

Yes, she could be caught and imprisoned. In fact, it was a likely possibility.

Yes, she had little idea of where she was going.

Yes, this entire expedition could be considered very foolhardy.

But she was stepping forward anyway because there was no other choice.

Father was a week or two from death, so the Attendants said. Even if she procured the seal and managed to copy it, and Anlyn managed to barter that copy without the people of ill-repute turning on her, he could very well die before their escape.

Another terrible thought to face, so she set it aside. Renna couldn't change his fate if she panicked, no matter how truly tempting panicking was.

It was better to focus on other matters, such as the adventure of searching through the rooms around her.

She eased open one door, allowing light to enter the room. A long rectangular table filled most of it, with elegant chairs on either side. A private dining room? Possibly. Likely to have a seal?

After a moment, she shook her head. Seals were used on documents, so she needed to find a room with a desk and many papers. Perhaps an inkwell.

Perhaps.

Perhaps none of this will end favorably, and I will be executed in the morning for treason.

Renna increased the gentle tapping of her fingertips on the cool marble.

Another room filled with scores of books, but no papers outside of them. Her fingers itched to flip through the volumes, but she moved on.

No time. No time.

Still more rooms, one with many windows and plants, another with a pinola, a guitar, and a harp. Instruments that beckoned for closer inspection, as they were far finer than any she had ever seen. Although the pinola looked similar to the one at the Mender Sanctuary.

With a sigh of regret, she continued her search. Still more doors.

Still more of them were locked.

Was the seal behind one of them? Was this whole mission doomed to failure for such a simple reason?

Possibly.

Renna's tapping became increasingly frantic. If only the stone-cursed corset would allow her to breathe! Deep cleansing inhales would allow her to excise the frantic thoughts and allow calmer ones to enter, just as she had been taught to breathe through pain.

She nearly ran into another room, clutching at the doorframe. More books on shelves that filled every single wall. Before her were two arched windows at least ten feet high, both of them open. A gentle breeze whispered in, soothing her nerves. And—a gasp escaped her—a desk! Covered with papers, a small wax candle, an inkwell, various writing implements, and what seemed to be paint-brushes as well. To be fair, she could only assume it was a desk. Something had to be holding up all the clutter.

So royals don't keep their areas immaculate. Renna had heard as much from Anlyn, but it was quite another thing to see it for herself.

What would it be like to have this much clutter with no inspections? She chewed on her lip. Something about the room seemed welcoming. Familiar. The weapons on some of the shelves, the empty places. The scuff marks on the floor, left by the claws of a dog. Somehow, she knew it was a dog.

Renna crept in, lit the candle with a sconce from the hallway, then her feet carried her closer to the desk. With everything in such disarray, the owner would hardly be able to tell that she had investigated. She reached for a loose piece of paper on which penmanship flowed in loops and curls.

She set down the candle on a nearby shelf, then picked up more of the sheaves of papers, searching for a seal and scanning the contents in equal measure.

Such fascinating writing. So different from her own thick scrawl. One notebook held a list of words and phrases.

He is dying.

Clayshaping.

Priest of the Eternal.

I have much to lose.

Always we.

They spurred almost-memories within her, as though looking through a dim forest, waiting for the dawn to set all alight.

"I believe we're at the stage where you inform me of your purposes, my lady."

A soft shriek escaped Renna, and all the papers flew from her hands as she whirled around. Even more lightheaded now that she had been caught, she blinked rapidly, trying to bring the owner of the undeniably male voice into focus.

He was taller than her by at least a head, wearing a long black coat with long sleeves pulled tightly over his biceps. Ruffles emerged from each cuff and around his throat. Black pants, black boots. And a deep bronze, garnet-touched face with a short beard that was unmistakably the visage of Prince Jaricob. Warm green eyes swept over her. Not solely in the appreciative manner of others, although there was some of that, but more seeking. Wondering, the way one would study a star in the sky.

The way he had studied her earlier as she had slipped her fingers through his hair. That surprisingly soft hair…

Even now, he *saw* her more keenly than anyone ever had, even her parents.

Or he measures me for a hangman's noose. But she silenced the thought the instant it appeared. She could no more envision him harming her than she could imagine her own parents raising a blade to her throat. No, this royal, this man, would only assist her.

With every aspect of his being.

And that confidence raised a fresh shudder along her skin. Not of fear, but another feeling that Renna had only learned about from the book she had read on spousal pairing. A sense of deep connection, of desire fueling every part of her with heat and need.

A part of her knew she should question the feeling more, be far more skeptical.

An increasingly larger part of her didn't care.

He raised his eyebrows, thick and black, then stepped farther into the room, lighting more candles as he spoke.

"I assure you, you are in no danger at this moment."

More of that same voice—dry with humor and utterly ordinary, and yet she could not mimic it. It leaped around her mind, playfully dodging every attempt she made to capture it. It sang to her soul, a welcome sound her ears had waited far too long to hear.

She nodded, managing a few words. "I know."

"Yes, you do, don't you?" The prince lit a final candle, then stepped toward her, as though he were stalking a wild creature. "Who are you?"

Renna swallowed. What harm could it be to tell now?

Somehow, she felt he already knew.

"Corenne M'Val—Corenne Valtor of the Sanctuary."

"Aha, yes. Corenne, called Renna. That . . . I knew that." He blinked as if confused, then nodded. "How could I know that? I've never met a Mender. But I've met you."

"Why haven't you met a Mender?" The royal family had their own private Sanctuary.

His mouth thinned and he tugged at one sleeve. "A complicated situation. Let us merely say that I am not in need of your assistance."

"Oh." She tilted her head. "Does Mending not work on you?"

"No, it doesn't." He sighed. "My turn for a question. Why are you here?"

The words spilled out of her, eager to seek the air. As if he didn't already know. *This, he doesn't know.* "I'm searching for a royal seal."

"So, you mean to steal it?"

"No!" Renna stepped forward as well, suddenly intent to have him know the truth. "Never. Only to make a copy and sell it."

Disappointment flashed in his eyes. "Ah, so much better."

"It isn't stealing!" Stealing was wrong. She wouldn't do that. "I am removing no objects from the palace. And I wouldn't be selling it myself."

"Hmm, so that's how an excuse sounds from someone else." The prince's lips quirked. "Although your accent says it with far more authority."

"Well…" Her mind went blank. "Likewise." Likewise? What did that even mean? Fool! Was there something else to say? Oh, yes. "Your Highness."

He made a brushing-off gesture. "Worry not over that. You've already come into my private study. I would say that earns you the right to call me Jaric."

I have that right because you are mine.

Her heart pressed her to move forward—then also pressed her to stay. She needed to touch him. She needed to find the royal seal and escape.

She needed to breathe. After a moment, Renna found the air to speak.

"Why should an invasion entitle me to anything?"

"Because you're—" Bafflement crossed his face. "I'm not certain. And it's rare that I'm not certain, which makes all this rather puzzling." He gave her another once-over with that sense of respectful evaluation. How was she meant to respond to that? As with his tone, his mannerisms seemed impossible to mimic or mirror, leaving Renna with only herself and her intentions.

It was an invigorating yet lonely feeling. Perhaps she truly was a star in the sky with so much distance between herself and others. Chasms of vast nothingness.

Emptiness.

If I could only be nearer to him, I would be filled.

"Why are you on this grand adventure for the royal seal?" His eyes winked down at her. Had he moved closer, or had she? Either way, they orbited each other now, only a few inches apart.

It seemed utterly natural, despite never having been so close to anyone outside her family. Renna wet her lips, trying to summon the words. Would he understand her plight? This prince, this Jaric, who had never been to the Sanctuary?

Yes, he would. He must.

"A complicated situation," she answered at last. "And a matter of life and death."

"Suitably drastic and suitably vague." He tugged at his sleeve again, his fingers near her dress, almost brushing the fabric. "Are you certain you cannot tell me? I am not a guard to be won over with a pretty smile."

Was that hurt in his eyes, a sharpening in his tone? Perhaps she should confess to all—but she couldn't, could she? She barely knew him, and yet all she wanted to do was lose herself in Jaric's arms at last and forever.

However, she also barely knew Anlyn, and Renna had trusted

her a great deal. So perhaps that reasoning was not so useful?

"It wouldn't be wise."

"You sneak into a restricted part of the palace to steal the royal seal, neglect to see that I have followed you the entire way, and you speak now of wisdom?"

He had followed her? Eternal help her, she was doomed.

Renna stared up at him, the odd attraction fizzling like the tonic they used to treat her wounds at the Sanctuary. Her hands itched to trail up his arms, to see if his biceps truly were that large, his jaw that strong.

Yes, very doomed.

What was she supposed to tell him?

He gave a short laugh. "Well, I cannot allow the royal seal to fall into the hands of an evasive, vagrant Mender, as intriguing as you are. Untold harm could come from this bartering you speak of, and as little as my family thinks of me, I will not endanger them or my country without good reason."

The bottom fell out of her stomach. And so it came to this. Renna had failed. The words echoed numbly within her.

She faced the pain, the grief of knowing this was all for naught.

That somehow, his answer had failed her. Though that made the least sense of all.

Her throat was thick when she spoke. "So, am I to be arrested then?"

"Hardly." Jaric frowned, almost touching a tendril of stray hair from her head. Her breath caught as his fingers neared her bare shoulder—but then moved away. But his eyes never left hers. "I would sooner arrest a rare jewel-wren."

His words filtered through the haze, stopping her cold.

"A jewel-wren? You think to cage me?"

Surely he wouldn't. Yet what other answer was there?

He blinked. "Well, not as such—"

"It is too late, Your Highness. For you see, I am already caged in the Sanctuary and there is no escape. And you are of no help to me, no matter how well you look." Her voice dripped with a sudden, cold venom. She stepped away from Jaric—no, the prince. He was no different from the other royals, or anyone outside the Sanctuary who wanted Menders to give every bit of their lives, and have nothing in return.

Even though he had never used a Mender's services, he would still know about what happened to Menders. He knew, yes, he knew, and he did nothing.

No one did anything. She'd tried, and she'd failed.

She wasn't strong enough to fight. She wasn't clever enough to reason.

And she could not mimic Jaric.

His eyes widened. "My lady Corenne, you are wrong."

"I tried, and I've failed. I've failed at everything, and it doesn't matter—"

A strong hand gripped her wrist, enough to still her thoughts. "I might be ignorant of Menders, but I am not so of you. I would help you with everything I have. How do you so quickly forget?"

His fingers sought to trace her cheekbone. "How quickly have *we* forgotten?"

Renna stared up into his face once more, seeing, knowing the truth there and feeling it resonate with her soul. Words flowed from her. "Forgive me. So many have taken from me."

"Yet I never have." His words matched hers in evenness and calm, even as he took her in his arms. Such sturdy, reassuring arms that sent heat rushing through her veins. "And I never will."

Stubbornly, she fought for reason. "Those words in your notebook. How could you have known?"

"Known what?"

"They were mine. They are mine."

"I know, the same way you know." He swallowed, nerves battling with need in his eyes. Those nerves undid her last defense. There was no defense against that honest confusion, that underlying devotion. "I am yours."

For what could she have against him? No more than Jaric had against her.

"I am yours," she murmured back.

His face closed the last few inches, his mouth pressing against hers firmly but gently, seeking only as much as she would give.

I give you all.

Her hands grasped his arms, and she stood on tiptoe to deepen the kiss. He groaned and pulled her close to him, his fingers traveling up and down her back.

And as one, their souls awakened.

As one, they *knew*.

"You nearly missed me."
She laughed, relieved
He suddenly knew
The shape of her form
As peals escaped her
Shadow and mist
Still curled around them
But now
There was substance
There were her deep blue eyes
Her shy, teasing smile
The soft gleam of her hair

"You accuse too quickly."
He laughed, relieved
She suddenly knew
The lines of his face
As a grin curved there
Shadow and mist
Still curled around them
But now
There was movement
There were his swift, sure legs
His quick, mocking smile
The bright flash of his teeth

And for all their troubles

All their struggles
They knew
They would never
Be parted
For they
Were
Single-souled

CHAPTER EIGHT

He couldn't think, could hardly breathe for the taste of her. The feel of her in his arms at last. After so long, after so many nights of mere moments of contact, their essences mingling in that shadowy netherworld beyond sense or true awareness. Awakening with no more memory than wisps and urges without reason, other than they were *right*.

All he wanted—all he craved—was to hold her indefinitely. No matter how absurd that seemed, it was necessary. It was everything.

A resonant ringing, at once melodious and unwelcome, traveled through the open door and echoed off the walls around him, shuddering through the precious woman he held in his arms. As one, they broke away from the kiss, lips parted, desiring more.

"The announcement for the Midnight Waltz," he said, answering her unspoken question.

"Is it already midnight?"

Jaric shook his head. "No, it cannot possibly be…" He glanced at a timepiece on the nearest wall, his neck muscles stiff. The numbers presented were even more odd. "Eleven forty-five . . . No. That's impossible. It was only ten when I entered."

"Maybe the timepiece is broken?" She twisted to look at it, a small popping coming from her spine. She was stiff as well. He pressed sore lips together. What had happened to them?

A knock sounded just outside the partly open door. Jaric heard a guard clearing their throat. In his arms, Renna seized. Jaric eased her behind him just enough to calm her discomfort.

"Yes? Who goes there?"

"Your Highness? The king and queen request your presence at the Midnight Waltz on no uncertain terms. They also bade me to clearly say that you were expected to dance with a 'suitable candidate,' according to their precise terms."

Jaric sighed. "I understand." He sought for a suitably vague, appeasing reply. "Inform them I will be there momentarily, as requested."

"I shall."

He waited until the guard's footsteps had faded, then turned to face Renna. She had backed up to the nearest wall of bookshelves, her hands clasped tightly together.

Renna tilted her head. "A suitable candidate..." Realization dawned on her heart-shaped, disarming face. "I remember. Your deal with them to find a bride by tonight."

"A deal I made only because I knew you awaited me. Somehow, I knew." He walked toward her again, careful to be slow. He was deeply aware of how unfamiliar, how uncomfortable she was outside of the Sanctuary. He'd felt her dread as if it were his own, in that mysterious place of knowing between falling asleep and waking once more. Between dreams and nightmares.

This time, she moved toward him as well, the tension in her

body loosening. "I want to know how this is possible, but more than that, I want…" Her eyes settled on Jaric. "I want to do as we planned."

"As we planned?" Even now, saying the words seemed ridiculous. No matter how true they were. "As we spoke of in our dreams."

"Yes." She exhaled, seeming equally baffled. "The plan to help my father and I escape."

"Stealing the royal seal wasn't part of the plan."

Her face tinted pink. "Yes, well, that was Lady Anlyn's idea when she took me to her estate today. She thought we could use it to barter—"

"With the men of ill-repute." Jaric frowned. "It isn't a terrible addition to our strategy, but had you let me know, I could have brought it with me. Procured some travel papers of my own, without the difficulty of stealing."

"Yes, but the Royal Fellowship Ball was tonight. I had to meet you tonight."

"Hmmm. It's still not the best plan."

He scowled at the bookcase as if it somehow held the answers to all these mysteries. It didn't, of course. Jaric had read every book twice over, at the least.

"I didn't know of any better options," she said, arms crossed over her chest. "I still don't understand. You wrote those words in your notebook. There are more of them. Yet I only—I only remember you from now. After we kissed. Then I knew."

"You didn't remember upon waking?"

"No. Never."

Jaric studied her, amazed that she accepted him, even when— "How? I don't understand."

But he should. He should be able to figure all of this out.

A hand touched his arm, light as a feather. He glanced down to see Renna beside him. "Your parents await your presence."

"*Our* presence."

Her shoulders slouched. "I doubt I am a suitable candidate."

"You are more than a suitable candidate, you are the only candidate." He smirked, tugging at an errant lock of her hair, the disheveled strands still silken to his touch. "But I will not put you in a place of harm. We can sneak out of a side door—I know the perfect exit."

At least that preparation had done some good.

Her face pinched with worry. "But you just told the guard you would be at the Midnight Waltz momentarily."

"A lie."

She squeezed his arm harder. "You shouldn't have done that."

"Better to lie than to lose you."

Renna's face softened. "And I you."

"And you're one to speak of lying." He quirked an eyebrow.

She blinked far too innocently. "I'm sure I have no idea what you are referring to."

"Who did you tell the carriage driver you were?"

"Well . . . I could have been Ria of Gheren." She stuck her chin out, hands on her hips, a pose that did jaw-dropping things for other parts of her figure as well. "My mother loved calling me Ria, and we lived near Gheren."

Her voice trailed off, a sudden sadness drawing her features into quiet shadows. Jaric's heart tightened and he grabbed her hand.

"Come then, she-who-could-be Ria of Gheren. Let us go before your tongue flies away with more words-that-are-not-lies. Only complete untruths."

With a wink that melted some of the grief from her face, Jaric pulled at her hand, leading them out of the room and down the hallway. A confident nod and a curt word handled most of the passing servants' curiosity, and a few coins in the pocket did the rest. Guards were sworn to never accept bribes, but that had never seemed to include Jaric, for reasons he'd never thought to question.

A thought flashed in his mind: Renna, speaking to Gerit in the main ballroom. Convincing him to allow her into the royal wing of the palace. Mimicking his speech, his small movements, just as Jaric did now, had done for a while, almost unconsciously.

Yet how could it be the same?

Her hand squeezed his arm again. Somehow, she had found her way to his bicep. Not that he minded at all. "Jaric? Which way do we go next?"

They stood at the intersection of two hallways. The right wall was adorned with a tapestry of the fall of Theolos Searlen, Duke of Motarn, in battle. The other was an elaborate embroidery of cats and chickens at play, of all the nonsense.

He turned toward the cat and chicken tapestry. "This way and through the kitchens."

A perfect opportunity to use his secret entrance. A time like this had been bound to come.

"Halt!" The voice of Fenklish, the captain of the guard, rang down the hallway. "Halt, Prince Jaricob Searlen the Tenth, by express order of their majesties."

Renna gasped, her hand falling away from his arm. He caught her hand in his. They would not be separated, not after finding each other. Not when there was still so much they didn't know. Besides that, Renna's father lay dying in the Sanctuary.

"A change of plans. This way!"

Pivoting, he raced toward the guards. Their eyes widened with surprise—all the better to push past them. Not even Captain Fenklish would think the reserved prince capable of such a stunt. All the better for Jaric.

Running down another corridor, he paused, Renna heaving great breaths beside him. Likely due to the stone-cursed corset because she otherwise seemed sturdy and capable enough. But until he could get her into more appropriate clothing—he quickly suppressed an image of her doing just that in his private quarters—she would have to endure. Right now, they needed to secure transportation.

And all the carriages were on the main drive, directly in front of the entrance to the ballroom.

There has to be another way.

Guards thundered down the passageway. Jaric clenched his hands.

No time. No time!

"Why not run straight through the ballroom?" Renna's words were quiet but sure.

"Through all those people?" And the Midnight Waltz was never stopped mid-dance. They would have to weave through all the dancers.

Her expression was wild with determination. "It worked with the guards. Do you have a better idea?"

The first flashes of guard livery of gold and blue tore around the corner.

"No."

As one, they ran toward the entrance to the ballroom, skidding past hallways, ducking to avoid more guards, and finally bursting through the doors, with Jaric—or Renna—giving quick apologies to Gerit and the others stationed there.

They shoved their way through the skirts of noblewomen and peasants alike, spinning around their starchly suited partners who gave cries of outrage. All of it was a blur before Jaric's vision, his eyes fixed on the door on the other side of the room, his hand inexorably anchored to Renna's.

Thirty feet. Twenty.

Fresh shouts behind him, likely guards demanding the capture of the wayward prince and his mysterious love.

For he did love her. There could be no doubt.

Ten feet.

He powered through the door, holding it open for Renna and releasing her hand to give her a chance to get to the nearest carriage. Whirling around, he shut the door against the guards who pressed in. It was only enough to startle and stop them briefly, but it bought him a few precious seconds.

As he ran to the carriage parked on the edge, something caught his foot, heavy and surprisingly soft. Some kind of animal? Jaric brushed off the thought and motioned to the driver.

"Take us out. Now!"

The white-wigged man dropped the bread he had been munching on. "Your Highness? Is this permissible by—"

"It is permissible by me." He shoved a heaping handful of alms-coins into the coach driver's hands. "Take us to Lady Anlyn's estate as fast as you can. There is no crime in visiting a member of the court."

The driver's mouth gaped.

"Quickly!"

"Yes, Your Highness!"

He swung himself into the seat, and Jaric bounded into the cabin area and settled next to Renna. He stripped off his outer coat, his shirt clinging to his skin with sweat. Renna fanned herself with her hand, her face glowing with exertion.

But she had made it. She had kept pace with him the entire way. This truly was the woman who, by way of their strange soul meetings, had shown her enjoyment of long trips into the wilderness with her father when she was a child. A warm pride and attraction flooded him. There could be no other maiden for him, runaway Mender and all.

Guards raced out the front entrance. At that moment, the horses leaped forward into a brisk trot, and then faster, the gardens speeding past the windows. Jaric leaned forward and stared out the window at the gate ahead. The guards would be signaling the gatehouse, trying to make the guard on duty close the gate.

His muscles tensed, and he gripped Renna's hand again. If the guards succeeded, he would have to run and coax Renna to do likewise, no matter her fatigue.

The guards' shouts grew louder.

But to no avail. The carriage ripped straight through the entrance, just as the gates were starting to swing shut.

Relief shot through Jaric. At least the coachman was earning his keep.

Jaric leaned back against the seat and relaxed his hold on Renna's hand. She massaged her fingers with a rueful look. "As if my feet aren't sore enough."

"I'm sorry." He shrugged.

She glanced at him skeptically. "You are?"

"For your pain, yes. But I would sprain your hand pulling you to the other end of the kingdom to keep you from their clutches."

Renna's frown melted into a look of complete agreement.

"I as well—" The carriage skidded down the mountain road,

veering around a corner and flinging her into Jaric's arms. Exactly where she should be.

From the sigh that escaped her and the way she eased into his arms, no other words were needed. They never were, at times. Dimly, Jaric remembered moments where their souls had stirred and mingled without a single word being necessary. As they were now.

There was only the sheer contentment of closeness, of escaping together at last. Of her hair brushing his arms as her head drooped against his chest, her eyes shutting in sudden weariness.

A faint smile curved his lips. He could hold her like this forever. And when they found her father, when they found a way to escape the Sanctuary and palace for good, Jaric would do everything necessary to secure her hand, even as he already carried her heart, and she his.

The question was, would they leave the country or attempt to trick the royal family into allowing Renna to be his bride? As much as he would prefer the latter option for the elegance of it, their abrupt departure made it untenable. No, they would likely have to leave.

Leave the country without saying good-bye to Usilea. Keddyr. Or without taking his dog along with them. Jaric's heart twinged. Renna would have liked Opal.

Far too soon, yet far too slowly, they arrived at an ornate orange-and-red gate, gilded in rose-gold. He winced. An eyesore of ostentation, which matched what he had been told of the Lady Anlyn. Yet she had helped his Renna, and she would be assisting them in their escape, so he would endeavor to tolerate her.

A knock on the door interrupted his thoughts, and the anxious face of the coachman peered in. "You should depart, Your Highness. You promise no harm will come to me from this?"

"Go to Princess Usilea and explain the situation. She will give you leniency." Hopefully. Usilea was remarkably skilled at separating Jaric's rare scrapes from the unfortunate individuals involved in them.

He gently moved Renna off his chest and into a sitting position. She yawned, rubbing her eyes. Lines creased her face from pressing into his jacket and buttons. Jaric released a short, quiet laugh, evoking raised eyebrows from her.

"What is it?"

"Only that you are the most beautiful woman I have ever seen."

She looked down bashfully, rubbing at her collarbone. Then she caught sight of her fingers in the dim light. "My hands! Eternal help me, that dratted powder."

"You don't need it."

"I know," she said dourly. "No more than I needed that shoe."

"Shoe?"

With another one of those shy smiles, her eyes glinting, she raised one foot and wiggled her bare toes. Jaric looked down. The other foot was still encased in the fur-covered monstrosity of fashionable footwear.

"I see," he muttered. "Apparently, my idea that I had tripped on the corpse of a small, furry creature was mildly exaggerated."

"Only mildly."

She stepped through the open carriage door, pulling off the other shoe. After he descended, she handed him the offensive footwear with a sweet, flirtatious smile.

"What is this? A token of your affection?"

"This? No." Renna's smile faltered—was she aware of how beguiling she looked? Surely not, with how she stumbled over herself the next second. "But . . . I don't have pockets in this dress."

He accepted the castoff trophy with a smirk. "From what I've observed, dresses never have pockets."

"An oversight, and all the more reason you should help me out of it." She paused, and her face flushed a deep pink beneath the olive. "No, that came out wrong—forgive me, my words don't always…"

At that, Jaric couldn't hide the grin that stretched over his face. He offered her his arm. "Come, before you lose any more garments. Or would you like me to carry you?"

Her mouth dropped open. "Carry me? Um…" She must have caught the laughter in his tone, for she rolled her eyes. "No, thank you. I can walk just fine barefoot. Far better than with shoes." She huffed, gripped the edges of her skirts, and began quickly ascending the pathway, a toss of her head releasing long locks of hair to fall down her back.

Jaric spared her another appreciative look, then easily caught up to stride beside her. Despite her short stature, she walked very briskly, resolutely looking ahead.

All the better. Especially since the palace guards would not be far behind.

There was no time to lose.

He and Renna had to figure out a way to rescue her father and escape the country—or, at the least, escape this situation in Syrus. If their elusive midnight meetings had resulted in any exceptionally clever strategies, his mind hadn't revealed them. And Lady Anlyn's plan of using black marketeers to falsify travel papers was *not* clever. Jaric might not have any interest in leading or being a part of his family's kingdom, but that didn't mean he wanted to ruin that kingdom.

He frowned at the rich foliage that surrounded the pathway. If only they could marry and escape to the dukedom in the northeast. Renna would be at home in the wild lands, and Jaric could easily adapt. But his parents would never permit such a thing, not with Renna's status as a Mender, and they certainly wouldn't give her father a suitable resting place for his final days. From what Jaric knew of the Sanctuary through Renna's experiences, they were very set on their rules and order, even if that order harmed the people they were meant to protect.

Instinctively, he moved closer to Renna, the back of his hand brushing against hers. She glanced up at him in surprise, then gave a quick smile, the irritation gone from her face. She was easily annoyed, perhaps, but also easily forgiving. Another reason he enjoyed her company.

"We're nearly there," she said, nodding up ahead.

He followed her gaze to the house that loomed ahead of them. Three stories tall, twice as wide in all directions with many small courtyards and copses of fruit trees, and brightly painted in the fashion of the nobility. Lady Anlyn seemed attached to orange and red here as well, as the walls were painted more garishly than a sunset, accented with roofs as red as strawberries. And yes, more of the rose-gold on every single window.

The color scheme was enough to turn his stomach, particularly when brightly lit with torches and candles along the broad steps of the front portico. Jaric scanned it quickly, alert to any threats from the guards posted there.

Yet none moved from their stations. Indeed, the only figures who were moving appeared to be far more in danger of suffocating each other with their mouths. He shook his head. Lady Anlyn was known for her love of parties.

They should avoid this couple altogether. No good would come of attempting to interfere—and none of it was of interest to Jaric.

Next to him, Renna called out. "Anlyn? I've returned."

The pair paused and broke apart.

Jaric scratched at his beard and muttered, "Renna, it might not be—"

"I'm certain it's her!" she whispered back fiercely.

Suddenly, one of the figures stepped forward into the flickers of the nearest light.

"Jaric? What in all stones are you doing here?"

Shock filtered through him at the glare off a shaved head, the bronze-garnet skin, a bit more exposed around the partially unbuttoned collar of his fine shirt. Although he'd managed to keep his jacket on, which is more than Jaric could say of the other times he'd interrupted his friend's interludes.

"Keddyr?"

His friend cut Renna a sidelong look. "Who is this? Is Prince Recluse finally taking a lover?"

"I'm taking a—" Jaric paused at a sharp tug on his arm. He stared down at Renna's wide, fearful eyes. His voice lowered. "Keddyr is a friend."

Her words were sure as they were soft. "I see what you do not. He is not in his right mind."

"Oh, that could very well be so." Keddyr was a foolish gadabout, a winsome flirt about the court who had come into his title early. His parents had died from vein-flu far from the reaches of the Mender Sanctuary.

Keddyr walked a few more paces toward them. "What? Who is she?"

"She is of little concern to you." The light, singsong cadence of the words could only be Lady Anlyn. "Only a personal servant of mine whom I allowed to visit the Royal Fellowship Ball to catch a good time."

His friend's eyes were sharp in the dim light. "Your maidservant caught the prince. A most impressive feat." Keddyr's jaw worked and his expression turned dark, like a thundercloud over sunshine, all the more startling for its rarity.

"You should leave now, Lord Hitchley." Steel entered the noble-woman's tone.

But Keddyr only met her steel with steel.

"Oh, I have no intention of leaving. At least, not without the trollop who is seeking to ruin my friend's future."

CHAPTER NINE

Jaric's hand covered hers where she held his arm. Relief and assurance as certain as the mountains flowed from him.

Not today, said his expression, immutable green eyes hard and jaw set.

"Refrain from speaking, Keddyr," he said. "Your words are rubbish."

She rooted her bare feet into the cold pavement. She felt solid for the first time in over six years, with no stifling shoes suffocating her feet and forcing her arches into uncomfortable shapes. She was home, at last, with Jaric—and it would be even more so when they had freed her father.

"My tongue might be loosened from drink, but I know a trollop when I see one," Keddyr shot back. "And she must leave. Now."

Renna tilted her chin ever so slightly, asking if Jaric would speak. The prince only shook his head slightly and squeezed her hand again.

Keddyr was hers to confront. He had accused her, threatening her as though she didn't belong there. She had every right to speak for herself, for so Jaric had always encouraged her. A faint smile twitched her lips. Her prince had always preferred what he called an "economy of energy." Why should two shout when one could do?

Still, she was relieved and anchored by his strength next to her.

Together, they would escape this place. Together, they would find a life of their own, far away from those who would cage them in and deny them each other.

Keddyr's voice reached her ears, loud against her and Jaric's quiet communing of souls. "Are you then deaf? Is that the ailment you are healing from, wasted woman?"

"When the words belong to a fool, then I am deaf." She turned to face her accuser who named himself Jaric's friend. "For why would I listen to a man who slanders me without reason?"

"I have much reason." He stalked closer to the edge of the portico, his face creased with anger. Did his legs sway slightly? "Jaric has made vows to his King Father and Queen Mother to choose a bride and live in seclusion. I may not agree with his parents, but I will not see my friend dishonor himself by breaking that vow."

Renna's insides quaked with fear and anger, enough that she, too, managed one step forward. "He vowed to me first!"

A laugh rippled down the steps. "Did he now? How can this be, when he has never mentioned a lover?" Hurt flashed across Keddyr's face. "And who else would he mention such a young woman to, except me, who he counts as a favored older brother?"

At that, Jaric spoke up next to her, his voice even and sharp. "As you mentioned your engagements with the Lady Anlyn to me?"

"Her? Oh, she's just…" Keddyr's voice wavered in time with his legs as he glanced over at Anlyn. Her face was tight in the moonlight, her mouth pinched in expectation. At once, Renna knew that expectation, perhaps from months of carrying Anlyn's physical pains and injuries.

She genuinely cared for this drink-addled man, though he was nearly ten years her junior. And she expected rejection in turn. Maybe that was all she expected, for while an older man marrying a younger woman was common, the reverse was looked upon with disfavor, or so Anlyn had confessed to Renna. And yet, men of Anlyn's age would not consider her hand, for they were only captivated by fresh youth and the pursuit of more children.

"She's just..." Keddyr gave an unsteady turn, his expression slack with unspoken thoughts. Or perhaps no thoughts, depending on how much he had imbibed.

Anlyn made a scoffing sound. "Come now, Keddyr, you'll make a scene, which is beneath you. Let us go inside before the palace guards arrive."

He blinked at her owlishly. "Ana, you are..."

Keddyr's foot caught on the edge of the step, and he careened to the ground.

"Keddyr!" Jaric and Anlyn shouted at the same time.

The nobleman flung out his hands to catch himself on his palms. They failed. His head hit the ground with a crack and he went still.

Silent.

Renna's stomach twisted. She followed Jaric's racing footsteps to his friend's side. Anlyn already knelt over Keddyr, patting his face and murmuring urgent words of comfort and remonstrance, with "you adorable fool" being a repeated phrase.

Jaric fell to Keddyr's other side, shaking him gently. "Keddyr, you hopeless miscreant, wake up."

Blood seeped from a wound on the side of Keddyr's forehead. He winced and groaned, but his eyes remained tightly shut, and his brown face grayish-tinged.

Renna's mind immediately snapped into focus. She stared at him fiercely, willing her Mender ability to analyze all that was wrong with him in order to fix it. Tension filled her as she braced herself for the onslaught of Receiving his injury—for so she would.

Must I, though? No one was forcing her to heal. To carry the ailments of this man who had repeatedly insulted her, even though he'd never met her.

How was it fair?

Renna. This is not the way. The stern words filled her mind in a voice that sounded almost like her father's, but not quite. Perhaps it was muddled by memory.

Regardless, they pierced her through.

She had been given a gift. No matter how that burdened her, she would not leave someone to die when she could Receive their wounds and save them.

Renna focused on Keddyr anew.

Nothing filled her senses.

No understanding of his wounds, no additional guidance about what ailed him. He remained as blank to her as a well-washed slate.

Her mouth dropped open.

"Jaric, I can't—"

"Not now, Renna!" Pain wrenched her prince's tone as he beheld his friend. "I must stop—I can't let him suffer like this." His voice lowered. "So much suffering, blood flowing in the wrong direction. Dizziness, nausea…" Jaric swallowed hard. "Such pain."

Her mouth dried like the plainlands in autumn before the mineral rains. There was something eerily familiar in the piercing way Jaric studied his friend. Almost as if…

But it couldn't be.

The only thing that prevented a Mender from healing an injured person was if another Mender was Receiving that injury first.

Wetness streaked Anlyn's face. "We should move him."

"No!" Jaric inhaled sharply. "It will only make his wound worse."

Renna sucked in a breath for strength and boldness. "Jaric, how do you know that?"

"I don't know. It doesn't matter." Jaric gripped Keddyr's hands tightly as they lay limp in his own. "Keddyr, tell me what I can do. I'll do anything. You're not allowed to die." His words turned as solid as iron, laced with the same intensity that Renna had used in so many healing rooms. "You're not. Allowed. To die."

With the final words, the air crackled with an all-too-familiar feeling of transferal. Renna's skin prickled and her blood raced like water down a steep embankment. Jaric, a Mender? *He can't do this. He's had no training, he's not ready—he can't possibly be!*

Moments flew by as swiftly as swallows, as slowly as the summer sunset, as inevitably as the tidewaters. All she could do was wait and catch him as he fell after Receiving for the first time.

The first time is always the hardest. We never heal such a serious injury on the first time.

She cradled Jaric in her arms.

At once, Keddyr's eyes flew open, his cut drying to a crusty dark red and his face rapidly gaining brightness.

"What in all stones?" He scrubbed a hand across his face. "What just happened?"

"You fell," Anlyn said, relief in her voice as she cradled his face. "A very bad fall."

"So . . . I am at the Sanctuary now?" Keddyr glanced around. "Did a Mender heal me?"

"No. Prince Jaricob did." The words fell from Anlyn like frozen rain.

Renna's arms ached from holding the full weight of Jaric's muscled torso. Weight she gladly bore as he sank into the deepening sleep of the first healing, his eyes shifting rapidly beneath closed lids.

It all made sense. How Menders were ineffective on him. How they had been drawn together—hadn't her father mentioned meeting her mother in a similar way, in the shadows of slumber and mystery? Renna reached for the memories but they slipped through her mental fingers. At the time, she had dismissed them as the joyful, fanciful tales of parents.

Now, she only had more questions. Question upon question. Part of her longed to burst through door of the Sanctuary and demand answers.

I am not leaving Jaric's side.

Distantly, she was aware of others helping her carry Jaric to a spare room near the back of the estate. They laid him on a bed, and she bade them bring water, some healing potions to ease symptoms, and for quiet. Jaric would need it—and so would she. The events of the night weighed heavily on her shoulders, fogging her hearing. She only had attention for Jaric. Only room in her mind to alternate between worry and prayers to the Eternal.

A hand rested lightly on her shoulder. She flinched as though burned, and the hand removed itself.

"Renna," Anlyn's voice came through the fog, clouded and unsure. "Do you need anything?"

Did she? Renna sought for an answer in her mind, as though through a murky, sticky swamp. The sort she had tramped through in the summer at her home.

A strange, sudden longing filled her. Not for her home—that

had passed away.

For freedom. For a chance to make a new home with the prince who lay before her on the bed.

"Renna?" Gentle. Insistent.

"I need to know. To understand . . . how he is like this."

"I'll do my best to learn what I can." That was Keddyr. Sluggish anger filled her. Keddyr the fool, who had behaved so foolishly and risked her Jaric. "What else?"

"I need…" She yawned. Past midnight now, was it? Her limbs were boulders as she sank onto the bed beside Jaric and curled up next to him. "I need . . . to rest…"

More words came from them, but they could not sever the shadows of her weariness.

Nothing could.

She was lost.

She sought him out
In the mist
In the shadows
That once sheltered them both
Now twisting and turning her steps
On unstable paths
Concealing her love
Concealing her soul
"Where are you?"
Her voice disappeared
Into the darkness
A depth that would have quailed her soul
In the world outside
But this was her world
Hers and his
And she would not let him be hidden
No matter how the pain gripped his words in icy ropes
"Where are you?"
Yet he had never been one for words
Now, they came not at all
The knowing sank within her
So she reached out
With heart, with soul,
With every breath and every bone
Treading the shadowed paths
And darkened ways
Until at last

Met By Midnight

Her fingers found his
Once more
He was buried in weariness
Marred with pain
Yet never
Ever
Alone

CHAPTER TEN

Jaric awoke to tightness in his head and softness at his side. He moved his hand to his head hesitantly, his touch revealing some kind of cloth around his forehead. Bandages? His head felt as fragile as the blown glass spheres that Usilea collected in her chambers. Next to him, atop the blankets that covered him, lay the source of the softness—Renna, her heart-shaped face pinched with worry even in sleep, and her hair a dark, tangled mess about her face.

His lips tilted up slightly in a smile. With equal hesitation, he nudged the tip of her long nose. She wrinkled it a little, her eyes squinching around her nose. He nudged her nose again and observed the same reaction, with the addition of a small squeaking sound as she rubbed her face in the blanket.

His lips widened into a proper smile.

"Are you a Mender or a mouse?"

"I am neither," she answered, words muffled by the blanket. "I am a very tired Renna who . . . who..." Her head turned up enough to release a yawn, and she blinked up at him, her dark blue eyes round with wonder. "You're awake!"

"It appears so." Jaric rubbed the bandages again, the events from the previous night still vague shapes and shadows in his mind. He glanced around the room. Elaborately carved wooden furnishings and rich silk wall hangings were barely visible in the dimness, for the curtains were drawn and only a few candles were lit. "Where are we?"

Another yawn escaped her. "Anlyn's house—well, more precisely, in one of her secret guest houses on a secluded part of the property."

"Naturally." The court's most notorious woman *would* have such places.

"Thank the Eternal, none of the houses were taken. Apparently, none of them have been used in months, for she had to send a servant to dust and set the room in order." Renna pressed her palms into the bed, managing to push herself upright. The dress from the previous night was gone, replaced with simple, flowing garments of deep brown, cinched into place with a red bodice that rose to just below her collarbone. For all the simplicity, he thought her all the prettier. The woman from the Royal Fellowship Ball who could pass among royals without much notice could now hike through forests and dells with ease. The latter scenario was far more interesting to him than the former, although he would never complain about the lower neckline of the ball dress.

His gaze returned to her face. Her eyebrows were raised in curiosity, eyes studying him in sharp appraisal, as if seeking out danger.

"How are you feeling?"

He paused to measure the ache in his head, the cramps in his muscles, the dryness of his mouth, and the nausea in his gut.

"As though I had a long night of ale-drinking and then allowed that fool Keddyr to knock me down in sparring." A frown tugged at Jaric's lips. The statement was foolish because he rarely drank that much and would never seek out a sparring match the morning after.

Renna chewed her lip. "Well, what you speak is partly the truth. Keddyr is the cause of your pain."

"How? The last I remember, it was he who was drunk, he who fell to the ground…"

His body tensed with the memory of racing to Keddyr's side, demanding his friend stay awake and alert, demanding that he not die.

"Do you not see?"

"No. Should I?"

She tilted her head to the side. "I thought . . . well, you are clever enough…"

Now his tension was fed by annoyance. "What do you mean?"

"Nothing, only that . . . you have never been to the Mender Sanctuary, so you don't understand. How could you understand?" She curled up into herself. "Jaric, you Received Keddyr's pain, not only his head injury but the damage of his mild wine-poisoning. You took it all from him and into yourself. Such has been the way of Menders from when we first emerged from among ordinary men and women."

It was as though she had thrown a mound of stones at him, hitting his stomach. The world around him faded, even the dizziness and throbbing in his head. There was only the spinning of his thoughts as he tried to decipher the truth of her words.

A Mender? But how could that be true? Jaric was the opposite of a Mender. He was immune to their skills. How could he be one himself?

At last, he spoke. "How is this possible?"

"It shouldn't be. Mending is passed down from father to son and mother to daughter. None of the rulers have ever been Menders, at least according to the histories I've read." Worry pinched her face. "But it would explain why you cannot be healed. No Mender can be healed by another Mender. The injuries we take from others will not leave a scar, but our own wounds do, and can never be unmade."

She reached out carefully, lightly tracing one of the scars on his arm. "It may also explain how we found each other. I remember my father explaining how Menders find their spouses. Something about how they are drawn to each other in ways beyond the knowing of the mind when awake. As shifting mists and dreams, until all is revealed when the two met in person. Although, they were able to remember the dreams when they awoke." She paused. "For some reason, I couldn't." She glanced at him. "You could. That's how you wrote down my words on those pages."

"Yes, I could remember, in part." He frowned. "Were you given anything that might addle your mind?"

"There was this tonic . . . We were all required to drink it after coming into our gift at age sixteen. Once in the morning, once in the evening." Her face darkened. "Two years? They kept me from remembering you for two years?"

Her face was tight, likely echoing the anger within Jaric. Another mark against the Sanctuary.

"What else did he say?" he asked.

Renna shook her head. "I don't remember. It never truly occurred to me until after I started to remember our meetings. I was eleven when he told me of his courtship of my mother. I had no interest in boys. Well, except as objects to try and outrun in races and outclimb in the forests."

"Both reasonable entertainments," he said, his frustration lessening as he pictured a younger version of Renna tearing through the woods and up hills. "Well, we can ask him when we rescue him. Perhaps he will know how my condition occurred."

Besides his father not being related to him by blood, but such an idea was almost inconceivable. King Obrik was devoted to Queen Giala. Their love story was one of fable, as he had been horribly ill at the time of their betrothal, and she had faithfully nursed him back to health.

Myriad emotions passed over her face: surprise, joy, and then a sadness that slitted her eyes. "Yes. It would be good to speak freely with him after so many years. I only hope he is able to . . . to speak…" Her mouth worked and her eyes gleamed with tears. "The last I saw of him, he seemed so weak, as though his blood were as thin as water."

He took her hand in his, savoring the feel of her skin and offering what comfort he could. "Then we should not delay any further in rescuing him."

Jaric sat up in the bed. The stones that had hit his stomach earlier now assaulted his forehead, leaving his gut free to experience the full tumult and twisting that had only been hinted at earlier.

"Take care!" Renna grabbed his shoulders firmly and eased him back on the bed. Jaric felt as helpless as a babe, fighting the agony that consumed him.

"Injuries have . . . never caused . . . this much pain."

"The bodies of Menders heal more quickly from Receiving injuries, which means we have to endure a greater intensity of symptoms." She reached for a cloth that rested in a metal bowl on the table next to the bed and pressed the cool fabric into his forehead, wiping away his sweat and soothing the ache. "The fastest I know of anyone healing from Receiving this type of injury is ten hours."

"How do you know?"

She shrugged. "Once in a while, an Attendant would let words slip."

Jaric ground his jaw. Her father could be dead by then. Eternal help him, he couldn't be the reason Renna lost her only remaining family without even a parting word. "Perhaps you should go without me."

She dipped the cloth into the bowl again and continued tending his face with the scented coolness. "I can't."

"Why not? You know the ways of the Sanctuary." Through their mysterious bond, Jaric was aware that Renna had steadfastly learned every curving stairway and small alcove. Then he caught a glimpse of sunlight through the dimming curtains, and a realization struck him. "But it is daylight."

A small smile curved her lips. "Yes, it is only two hours from midday. By the time you are well, we may begin preparations to sneak into the Sanctuary."

He nodded, and immediately regretted it as pain flared through his temples.

"Besides, I can't face my father without you."

"You are afraid of him? For him?"

"Afraid of what I may find when I seek him." She set the limp cloth back in the bowl and sat up, curling her arms around herself once more. "If he lives, I want him to meet you before he passes on. If he is dead..." She stared at the bedspread, tracing invisible patterns in the yellow expanse. "If he is dead, I don't know if I will have the strength to leave his side without you there. And it would be easier to carry his body out between the two of us, so that he may be buried and set at peace with fevenias over his grave."

Jaric set his teeth against another wave of nausea and pain. "The traditional burial."

"Menders are denied this. The Attendants say we must pass through the flames."

"Burning? It isn't done."

"It shouldn't be done." Her tone turned low. "It will be made right for my father."

"Yes, it will." He studied her. "And then, no matter what happens, we shall be married."

A faint smile curled her lips. "Yes, we shall." Renna paused. "It was a noble thing, what you did for Keddyr." She spoke slowly, as if not convinced herself.

"I didn't know what I was doing."

"But if you had known, you would have done it anyway."

"Of course," Jaric said. "I couldn't have let him die."

"I could have." Her words were a whisper. "After years of Receiving without a choice, when it was given to me . . . I didn't want to heal him, Jaric. Well, I did, and I didn't."

Jaric fought through the pain, trying to grasp what she meant with her words. "He'd insulted you."

"Is that an excuse to let him suffer?"

"Maybe not. But it is a reason for your hesitation."

At that moment, a whisper of wood and a creak of metal interrupted them. Jaric winced against the oddly deafening sounds. Renna rose from the bed, leaving an empty space. Now and forever her space. A few more voice-like whispers, then she entered his field of vision, holding a small vial filled with burnt-orange liquid.

"What is that?"

She sat close to him on the bed, uncorking the vial. "One of the best pain-relieving syrups from the Sanctuary."

Jaric eyed the vial with equal parts suspicion and hope. "How did you get it?"

Renna took a metal spoon from the small bedside table and dripped the orange liquid into it. "Lady Anlyn seems to have her ways. I would never have thought the Attendants were vulnerable to such blatant bribery, but she continues to prove me wrong."

"So it appears." The lady seemed to have a number of other sides to her besides the brash court tease.

She turned to him, spoon raised before her. "This will make you sleep, but that will only help you heal more completely."

He breathed through the fresh stirring of skepticism that twisted his stomach. "And you have taken this remedy yourself?"

"Yes, particularly when I have Received terrible internal injuries."

"I don't like that you Received those."

Renna sighed. "I didn't enjoy it either, but I had no choice. And it is my gift."

A fresh thought pushed at him. "Yet is not your life also worth saving? If you Receive too many injuries, what does that do to a Mender?"

"We die too early." Her answer was flat and barely audible. "Now please, take the medicine. It tastes like coppermint, so it should go down easily, and it will take hold fast."

"Yes, my lady." Jaric opened his mouth.

The solution soothed the dryness of his mouth and slipped smoothly into his stomach. A few spoonfuls later, both the room and Renna faded from view. Thank the Eternal, so did the pain.

The next thing Jaric felt was a deep emptiness in the pit of his stomach. He tried to open his eyes but found them crusted over with sleep sand. He swiped at it, his motions stiff, but far less painful than they had been earlier. However, the actions did little to assist him in seeing, for the room was now fully dark.

Another whisper of wood and a creak at the door. Jaric turned his head to face it.

"Who's there?"

There was a scuffling sound and a crash of metal on stone. He bolted upright, muscles tense, hand reaching for the knife hidden at his side. Nothing. His pulse raced. *Renna.*

A load of fur and claws and licking tongue piled on top of him.

"Opie?" The dog whined and whuffled at his chest. Jaric chuckled, petting the labordrim's scruffy fur. "Get off me, you absurd dog. Who let you in here?"

"Eternal's teeth, Jaric!" The curse rang out in the room. Jaric relaxed. It was only Keddyr, who loudly continued, "You alerted that dog, and she upended everything. Now I've had to send a servant for more water and ale. Are you well again?"

Jaric opened his mouth to respond, but Keddyr's words continued in tandem with the lamps in the room being lit, illuminating patches of his friend's open expression.

"You've been asleep for over ten hours. I was worried, but your Mender woman insisted it was to be expected from a first Mending, that they were harder than the rest." Keddyr picked up a tray of food from a table near the door and walked over to Jaric, his expression fierce and concerned. "Of course, there is the question of how you were able to Receive my injury. My first thought is infidelity on the part of one of your parents, which might explain why you and Lea look so different."

"Our features are similar, my parents would never," Jaric managed to cut in. His tone was flatly dismissive, belying the anger that fired within him.

Opal settled next to him, her gaze fixed on the food. So much for the love of a faithful animal companion.

Keddyr set the tray on the table beside the bed and raised an eyebrow. "Wouldn't they, though?"

If the words had been anything more than a simple question, Jaric would have been tempted to punch his friend in the jaw. But the truth was, Keddyr knew more of the gossip and intrigues of the court than Jaric ever would. *And I barely know my parents, as well.*

He knew the side of them they showed the public and the court, with perhaps a bit more affection in private. King Obrik had ensured that Jaric was properly trained in physical and mental capacities, and his mother faithfully ordered etiquette and decorum tutors for Jaric's royal education. But it had always been Usilea they confided in, especially when she had reached the age of fifteen. Since then, Jaric had seen the distance all the more, even in Lea's gaze, although very reluctantly.

She had mentioned secrets earlier. Was this what she had meant? His mind spun. *Lea, what were you told?*

"I don't know," Jaric finally admitted. "It appears I know much less than I ever realized."

"Yes, well, I'm sorry about that." Keddyr drew up a chair to the side of the bed. "I assure you, I knew nothing of this either. And I..." He swallowed. "I would never have asked you Receive all that stone-cursed trouble from me."

Jaric shrugged. "You're my friend. You aren't allowed to die."

"Neither are you," Keddyr shot back, his brown eyes blazing. "Mending may have originated from a man laying down his life for his friend, but that is not your place. Understood?" He gripped Jaric's shoulder tightly. "I have so few true friends."

Jaric held his gaze firmly. "I have one. You."

They stared at each other for a moment. At last Keddyr sighed and pulled away with a final smack to Jaric's shoulder. "You would think I could lecture someone six years younger than me."

"If you would like, I can assure others that you tried." Jaric smirked. "Although they may not appreciate you lecturing the prince."

Keddyr gave a short laugh. "Considering we've knocked each other down countless times in the ring, I doubt they will care. They're much more interested in gossiping about my relations with Lady Anlyn."

"Relations?" The savory scent of roasted meat and barley reached Jaric's nose, and thankfully did not turn his stomach. He reached for the bowl of food and began to eat, slowly at first, then more and more quickly as his appetite awoke, only pausing a moment to give a tidbit to Opie.

Keddyr watched him absently. "You might need to eat slower..."

"Says who?"

"Your Mender woman, who would have been here herself except that she honored my need to speak to you. She is busy finalizing a map of the Sanctuary for our mission to rescue her father."

"*Our* mission?"

"Do you think I would let you do this without me? As for Anlyn, I advised her not to involve herself. She advised me to respect my elders and honor the fact that she had been involved before I had." Keddyr shook his head and smiled. "So, what of this Renna?"

"We're betrothed, of course."

"Why 'of course'? I persuaded her to speak of your connection a little, but it makes no sense to me." Keddyr rubbed his hand over the skin of his head.

"I doubt I could do better." Jaric picked up a jar-apple from the table and bit into it, giving himself time to think. Everything seemed far too fanciful or farfetched to speak aloud. "We have been . . . meeting at night. In…"

"Dreams?" Keddyr scoffed.

"Akin to that, although . . . forget it." Jaric took another bite of the sweet, mellow fruit. "It is what it is. We know each other. We have known each other for a while."

"How long?"

He searched his mind. When had the meetings started? "Two years."

"Hmm."

"And we are going to marry as soon as her father is rescued, and they are both safe."

Keddyr stared at him. "She mentioned that you are going to leave the country."

"That was the plan, yes."

"Have you thought of what that will do to your sister?"

Yes, of course he had. Did everyone think he was stupid? Jaric turned to the third item on the tray, a type of goldfin and root soup, hot and blended smooth. "Usilea is capable and clever."

"She is young and inexperienced, and whether you're willing to admit it or not, she relies on you to be her strength."

Jaric's gut twisted. "I have been her strength as much as I'm able."

His friend glared at him. "You cannot be so selfish as to leave her."

Did Keddyr think this was easy?

Jaric met his stare. "Do you know what they do to Menders? What they have to endure? Because I do, from knowing Renna. I will not allow her or her father to live in that manner any longer. And what will the court say of me, a Mender hidden among the royal family?"

"True, but you cannot simply run away from your problems either. Not even into the arms of a pretty young woman in distress."

"So I should run into the arms of a woman ten years my senior?"

Keddyr paused, swallowing hard. "Anlyn is different. And what goes on between us is much less than the court rumors. We simply began talking at a party one evening. She was different than…"

"The young ingénues who desire your title and bed?"

"Yes. She plays the game of flirtation, but she doesn't . . . entertain nearly as much as the court assumes. She's strong, self-assured. Stable in who she is, able to challenge me. We found we were both lonely for quality conversation." He ran his fingers over his head again, his words quieter, more unsure. "What you saw last night was the first time we had ever embraced."

It was the truth, as far as Jaric could discern. Though he still had no reason to trust Lady Anlyn personally, besides the fact that she had sheltered Renna. "Hmm."

"Hmm?" Keddyr cracked a rueful smile. "I supposed that is the best I'll get from you for now."

"I could say the same of you, but it would mean you would stop talking. We both know that would never happen."

Keddyr wrinkled his nose. "Finish, misanthrope. You must be ready for the mission tonight. There is a dying father to rescue, and perhaps bury?"

The morbid turn settled Jaric's mind to practical matters. "No futile attempt to dissuade me?"

"Hardly. Not even your Renna suggested that, which is a sign she might know you well after all." His friend stood. "We leave in two hours. That should give you enough time to ready yourself and get any assistance you need."

"I will not need assistance," Jaric said stiffly.

"With any assistance necessary," Keddyr said with added emphasis and a glint in his eyes. "Including sparring warm-ups for whatever threat we might face. Renna assured me you would be healed, but remaining abed may have made your muscles quite useless. All the easier for me to win this round."

Jaric grunted and tilted his chin up. "You only wish."

Keddyr brushed him off diffidently. "Finish eating, clean up, and then prove me wrong. And none of your Mender tricks, either. Renna told me about your ability to read auras and mimic." He scrunched up his face. "Have you been doing that this whole time?"

"If I had, would I admit it to you?"

"Oh, I'm knocking you down extra for that."

Jaric turned his attention to his food and the adventure ahead. They were breaking into the Sanctuary. While Menders were steadfastly pacifists—or so the story went, even traveling to Jaric's ears—their Guardians and Attendants could be another matter.

Who knew what they were capable of?

He studied his dog thoughtfully.

"Opie, we're in new territory now."

She whined knowingly. He grinned and tossed her another bit of meat.

If he and Renna ran away, Opal was coming with them.

CHAPTER ELEVEN

Not long now. Not long now.

Renna's skin prickled despite the warm night and the even warmer folds of the Mender robes that swamped her skin in cold sweat. And here she had imagined casting the robes aside forever in her quest for freedom. Soon, soon she would.

But first, to rescue her father, whether he be living or dead.

Another chill shuddered through her at the thought. A hand took hers. She stared up into Jaric's cowled face next to her, his forest-green eyes as steady and firm as his hold on her palm. He was still coping with the revelation of being a Mender, yet he was willing to stand by her and do what he could to help her free her only remaining family.

She leaned her head against his shoulder. No matter what, at least she was not alone—and she never would be.

Truer words were never spoken. Her lips quirked of their own accord as she took in the two individuals sitting opposite them in the carriage. Anlyn was clad in an elaborate outfit of gleaming jewel-toned silks and draping sleeves, prepared to play the role of demanding noblewoman in her usual style. Her black hair fanned out in a glorious explosion of mindfully arranged curls. Next to her, Keddyr was clad all in black and wearing soft-soled shoes. He would wait in the shadows to assist with carrying out her father's dead body, if it came to that.

Eternal, please let it not come to that. Let him still be alive.

As they continued to descend through tree-lined streets to the main roads of Syrus, Renna reviewed the plan in her mind. Lady Anlyn would dismissively return Renna, claiming she required a fresh Mender to tend to her imagined ailments. While she made a suitably dramatic scene, Renna would allow herself to be led back to the Purification Cells, for the Sanctuary leadership would want to ensure her mind was properly cleansed from any outside contamination. Meanwhile, Jaric and Keddyr would slip over the wall that surrounded the Sanctuary and walk through the courtyard garden that was still under maintenance. Keddyr would remain there while Jaric would sneak into the main building of the Sanctuary, free Renna from the Purification Cells, and together they would go to the Room of Last Decay. After that?

A sigh escaped her. After that, it would depend on whether her father lived or died, and what condition he was in. He would certainly be even more wasted than when she had last seen him, though it was only a few days ago.

Renna gritted her teeth. *Barbaric!* Anlyn had exclaimed when she had learned the truth. Keddyr had agreed. Both of them declared they had known nothing of how much Menders suffered, how much of their lives were drained away. And they certainly didn't know of the compulsory aspect of serving in the Sanctuary.

If only I could do something to change that, to reveal the truth. To give others a chance at freedom.

She blinked at the turn of her thoughts. What could she do? She was the daughter of a priest, the wild Mender girl taken from her northern home and cloistered in the Sanctuary. She was no revolutionary, no brave and bold speaker.

And what harm would such unrest do to the Menders within the Sanctuary? They were raised to comply, not to resist. To insist that they suddenly be turned out could be horribly jarring and upsetting. What if they all chose not to heal as well? Was that truly the answer? Did freedom from coercion give Menders the right to allow others to suffer, even if it preserved the longevity of the Menders?

Too many questions. Who was Renna to decide the answers?

Yet the thought tickled at the back of her mind.

If only. If only.

If only I could free them…

Jaric squeezed her hand, and she amended.

If only we could.

Hadn't he said he was only an insignificant prince? His own parents were willing to exile him into the north, to the dukedom of Motarn. What sort of impact could either of them have?

The clatter of horse hooves on cobblestones shifted to a quiet patter as they turned onto the soft dirt driveway of the Sanctuary. It stood apart, sheltered from the rest of Syrus in a grove of tall tallowfeather trees, their long, frondlike leaves drooping over the three-story building.

Anlyn nodded to her. "It's time to remember who you are—at least for tonight."

"Yes." She lifted her chin. "For one more night."

"Only one more," Jaric rumbled.

He moved on the seat until he faced her, hands trailing along her jaw like she was made of morning dew and flower petals and other delicate things too soon dead in the passage of time and disease. Never mind that she had been considered more sturdy and able to bear hard Receivings, never mind that he knew of her strength. He still treated her with care.

She rested her hands on his upper arms and tilted her face up to his until there were only inches between them.

"Return to me soon, my love." Shock filled Renna as the words escaped her. Had she truly said that? For certain, their souls had joined at midnight in love, but to voice it aloud and in front of others? What was she thinking? She hadn't been thinking, not at all!

Her face flushed and her lips parted to stammer out an explanation—and then his mouth was on hers in a deep kiss that teased and warmed her from head to toe, chasing aside the cold fears within her. She melted toward him, pushing aside his hood, needing to know that she wasn't alone. That even when she vanished into the Sanctuary, he would find her.

See me. Please, see me.

At last, they parted. He studied her intently, then gave her a last peck on the side of her mouth, his short beard gently brushing her face . "I will, my love."

Renna's heart leaped at the words, at the way he held her close. The sound of a throat clearing jolted her back to the present, and she twisted around in her seat to face Keddyr. And was Anlyn hiding a smile? No, she wasn't attempting to hide it at all.

"If you two are quite finished, I have a grand performance of my own to give."

Jaric studied her. "Are you sure the servants at your house—"

"Will care for your dog? Yes, my dear prince. Goodness, you care for that creature as if she were fully human."

"And what of your cats?" he shot back.

"My cats are another matter entirely." She smirked, then gave her golden mantle a final tweak. "Shall we, Renna dear?"

Renna sighed and nodded. A small part of her wished she were back at the house with the cats and Opal. They would be better company than the Attendants she would face.

Father, I do this for you. Please, be alive.

The noblewoman's mouth set into a firm line. "Good. Let's see how much trouble I can make tonight."

"You'll do an admirable job," Keddyr said.

She glanced at him, tilting her head. "Are you saying this is one of my valuable skills?"

He picked at his collar and met her gaze evenly. "I should hope so. After all, your self-confidence is one of your most attractive traits."

Anlyn licked her lips, but she only said, "Always quick with the right answer."

"One of *my* most attractive traits."

"Along with your obvious modesty." She stood, signaling for the coachman to open the door. "And now, we depart. Renna, your footwear?"

Renna stared at the Mender shoes—not the ones she had worn to the Royal Fellowship Ball, but a fresh pair that Anlyn had procured from the Sanctuary through one of her many mysterious connections.

The heavy, cloth-wrapped shoes seemed to stare back at her, taunting her feet with imprisonment. The first step back into her old life of endless Receivings and healing periods, never to be free.

She couldn't do this.

Renna's stomach dropped to her knees, which shook beneath

the robes. What if she never returned? What if Jaric wasn't there? What if her father were dead, and her beloved couldn't find her?

I do not do this alone. I do not do this alone.

With a clench of her hands, she put on the shoes, wincing at the tightness. Horrible things. She followed the noblewoman out of the carriage and onto the narrow strip of wooden porch in front of the Sanctuary. Anlyn was already busy making a spectacle of herself in front of the two Guardians and their accompanying Attendants.

"Here she is!" Anlyn flung out her right arm with a flourish. "Returned to you, safe and sound of mind and body. Now, I simply require another Mender."

The Guardians stood straight and stiff beneath their robes. One said, "Lady Anlyn, Menders are not plaster wrappings for you to use and throw away at a whim."

"Oh, it is not a whim. A widow such as myself has certain afflictions of advanced age that must be seen to." She placed a hand over her heart. "Would you see me fall ill to the travails of my senior condition?"

The Guardian's light voice countered, "Your husband's death was truly tragic, but you are not of an age that should require a Mender staying at your estate at all, much less two nights in a row. Such a grace is unheard of."

"Even for one of my generous patronage?" Anlyn's tone remained singsong, but her eyes hardened. "A generosity that has enabled quite a few improvements to be made to your Sanctuary, dare I say in the personal quarters of the Guardians as well as in the general arrangements."

"Well, that is . . . that is to say…" The Guardian trailed off. "If you will excuse me, Lady Anlyn."

Renna smiled within the shelter of her hood. It was rare she saw anyone fluster the Guardians and Attendants so.

"Attendant A'Conshin," the Guardian added, "escort Mender Corenne M'Valo to the Purification Cells."

Her smile disappeared. She barely listened as the Attendant acknowledged the order and led her into the wood-paneled anteroom. The door shut and locked behind her with a dry click.

"See to yourself, Mender M'Valo." The Attendant gestured to a small alcove.

Renna suppressed a sigh. With measured steps, she entered the small space and doffed her outer robe for a fresh garment, and her shoes for a fresh pair. The first of many steps to cleanse her from any potential diseases or impurities.

She followed the Attendant down a narrow hallway to the left, and then another hallway, and a third. Farther and farther into the maze of corridors, away from the outer ring with the windows. Her shoulders tensed, and only years of training kept her breathing even.

Memories filtered through her mind. Of being led here between her father and mother, clutching their hands, terrified of the robed figures around her. Bewildered that they kept insisting Renna was here for her own safety and well-being when she had never asked to come, when her home in the northeast had never endangered her family.

Her throat tightened as the Attendant exited the main Sanctuary building and walked to a small field surrounded by another fence. The Purification Cells.

A key unlocked the gate, and the Attendant drew it open, bidding her to go to one of the small, square cabins. Within each was a small bed, a basin and sink, a copy of the third edition Mender edicts bound in leather on a small table, and a plain stool.

Chills trickled up her spine. This was where they separated

them. Renna in one cabin, her mother in another, her father in a third.

This was where Menders went during their initial processing, if they had the presumed misfortune to be born outside the Sanctuary. And this was also where they were reeducated if their devotion to their supposed divine mission wavered.

"Go, Mender M'Valo," the Attendant said, gesturing to her assigned cabin again. "Here you will wait until we release you."

Even as she obeyed, Renna chanted the truth over and over in her head.

She would get out.

She would get out.

This time, she would get out—without an Attendant watching her every move.

This time, she would be free.

What will I become when I am free?

She couldn't think about that right now.

As she entered the cabin, the door shut and locked behind her. Three steps forward to the bed. Two steps right to the table and stool. One step right and back to the basin in the right corner.

She had only spent a few days in a cabin. Some Menders spent weeks, even months, in here, seen only by their disciplinary Attendant and Guardian. Only allowed a few brief periods outside.

Renna pressed her palm into the smooth wooden wall, trying to imagine what it would be like if this were all she could see for so long. Day after day, night after night.

Most of the Sanctuary people would know no different. Each Mender eventually submitted, as far as she had been told. But did that mean they were hopeless? What if they didn't know better, just as Jaric had been blind to his own nature?

What if?

What if?

She tapped her fingers on the wall with each repetition of the thought, calling upon the familiar mind training. She calmed her thoughts, facing the fear that Jaric would not come for her, acknowledging it, and choosing to hope anyway.

Choosing to breathe, in and out.

In and out.

Innumerable moments passed. There was no sign of him.

Renna sat on the bed, pulling off the hateful shoes and tugging at the edges of her robe.

I will hope.

I will hope, though hope is shattered.

Maybe a broken hope, a broken dream, was better than no dream at all.

Eternal, how she hated being locked away.

I will hope, though hope is shattered.

She stared down at her hands, watching them sparkle with a few droplets from her eyes. She remembered the words of her mother. *Tears are not an evil, for they are your soul made visible in crystal mirrors. The only evil is holding them within to turn to soot and ashes like the mineral-rains, scarring your heart.*

More tears flowed down her cheeks. For the times she had been alone in this cabin. For the wasting away of her mother and the disappearance of her father into endless Receivings while Renna was trained and tested in solitude. For those who lived here, oblivious to how worthy, how precious their lives were beyond simply serving as a conduit for the healing of others.

At last, she sat there.

Utterly spent.

Until a voice spoke her name into the silence.

"Renna?" A whisper, rough and cautious and quick, yet for all that, caring. "We must go now. Time is short."

Her head snapped up.

Jaric stood there, robes clinging awkwardly to his form, his eyes dark and intense. Certain.

"You're here."

"Where else would I be?" His words echoed with impatience, but also warmth. "Come now!"

With no further hesitation, she leaped off the bed and grabbed him in a hug, holding fast to the truth of the moment.

He was here, and soon, no matter what happened, her father would be free.

She would be free.

Chapter Twelve

Renna held Jaric in relief, as a lifeline, burying her face into the robes covering his chest. He rubbed her back, pressing through the fabric to soothe and reassure. Relieved that he could be there for her but wishing for all the world he knew what troubled her.

Then suddenly he knew, as simply and completely as recovering his own memories. That place where their souls mingled allowed him such access, although he would never want to pry, especially now, when time was so short. Yet, for a moment, Jaric knew about Renna's time of surrendering to captivity, the days of isolation, the nights of loneliness and fear of the future. About hanging on to belief in the Eternal, even as it often withered to a thread.

Could that have been him? Was this what his parents had hidden him from? Jaric shook his head. They had only told him a lie that led to a different sort of isolation from others, a belief that he was tainted and a threat to the royal family's veneer of strength.

They still lied to the people, with no one the wiser. It rankled his soul.

But there was no time.

"I see you." He pressed a kiss into the top of Renna's head. "But there's no time right now."

"I know."

She pulled away, brushing at the streaks crusting her face. Tears. Had she been crying? An urge to hold her again almost overcame him, but she had moved beyond his grasp. With a few muttered words of frustration, Renna shoved her shoes back on—or tried to.

"Are these truly necessary?" she grumbled.

"If we want to pass unnoticed and escape, yes."

"Of course we do." She paused. "There is no other path but leaving."

She yanked viciously on the shoe, trying to force it on.

He knelt before her, taking the offending object from her hand. "Continuing like that will break your foot, or the shoe."

"The shoe would die first."

A smile twitched his lips. "Are you certain? It could be a very cunning shoe."

"It is no match for my wrath."

Amid her distraction, he managed to slip the back of the shoe over the heel of her foot.

"And yet, it has triumphed."

With a quick tug, he pulled her to her feet.

"Yes, because you aided it." She glared at him, then followed close behind as they exited the cabin.

A few quick steps and they were through the gate around the quarantine area. Jaric pictured the path to the Room of Last Decay from the layout Renna had drawn back at Anlyn's estate. The final resting place of Menders was surprisingly unhidden, but apparently the Guardians were so certain of the trained submission of their captives that they made little effort to conceal the room. Yes, it was situated belowground, down more mazelike hallways, but there were no guards, and even Attendants were scarce.

Soon they were closing in on the plain, unmarked door at the end of a long hallway. Next to him, Renna folded her hands together, wringing them within her sleeves. Jaric only increased his pace. Delay would help nothing. The sooner they found her father, alive or dead, the sooner she would find release from her tension.

He reached for the handle and gave it a slight tug to deduce whether he could pry it open or if he would have to force it open.

The knob twisted easily in his hand. Shock flowed through him like ice water.

Jaric backed away, pushing Renna behind him. Was someone inside the chamber? But even if there were, they should have locked the door. Renna had said the door was always locked.

But now it creaked open, leaving a gap that revealed a row of tables, each one seeming to hold bits of wrinkled skin, sagging flesh, and brittle hair, none of it forming whole bodies.

A shudder passed through him, even as his mind insisted the image was an illusion, that the tables indeed held fully intact people.

In any case, entering the room was unthinkable.

"A trap," he muttered, only for Renna's hearing.

"It matters not either way. We must find him." She pressed against the protective arm he held in front of her, urging him forward.

He held firm. "Not at the expense of losing you."

"Then don't lose me." Irritation filled her tone now, along with desperation.

Longing.

Jaric sighed. He had a bad feeling about this.

"Stay behind me."

Slowly he inched the door open with the tip of his shoe, while gripping the knife hidden beneath his robes.

Before him, the room opened up, perhaps thirty feet long. Smooth stone walls held candles flickering in iron sconces. Plain iron tables lined either side with a narrow aisle down the middle. Some of the tables were empty while others held old Menders, their bodies wrapped in thin, white shifts.

No, they were not old Menders, not as Jaric counted old age. Knowledge from his nights of meeting with Renna surfaced in his mind. Menders aged and died while still young. Perhaps they might last until their fourth decade, but never to their fifth. The official reason was that it was a natural consequence of their gift. No, it was the consequence of over-using that gift.

Jaric had recovered from his wounds on his own just fine. Others could do the same.

He moved closer to one table where a man lay, almost shrunk from weariness. Was this what his parents had protected him from? Being used for every last shred of healing? But why, when the king and queen could move to change the laws? Why wouldn't they do so?

Beside him, Renna sucked in a breath. He glanced down to see her gaze fixed on a table at the far side of the room.

"Father!" She ducked around his arm and raced to the table, her eyes wide with relief and fear. "He lives!"

Stones! Jaric followed her. "Someone outside could hear!"

Renna looked up from the table at his sharp words, her mouth dropping open.

"Someone already has." A new voice, yet as familiar to Jaric as his own face in the mirror. Quiet and sure, with an undertone of melancholy.

Usilea.

He turned around to face his sister. She wore the plain, dark clothes of a peasant, her hair braided and wrapped away from her face, washed to strange shadowy hues in the candlelight.

Jaric swallowed. "Lea? What are you doing here?"

"I could ask you the same question, considering this room is highly restricted." Her voice was quiet, controlled. "You must leave now, before our parents discover you."

His mind raced, trying to understand his sister's reaction. There was no surprise, no disbelief—only worn resignation. Usilea knew of this place. She knew what was being done to Menders.

She knew and had told him nothing.

"Would you deny me the knowledge of my own fate, dear sister? And that of my beloved?"

Her lips pressed together. "So, you know."

He expected her betrayal to hurt less. But it didn't.

"As you have for years." Jaric gripped the knife tighter, holding it out in front of him. He would never harm his sister. But he would also not allow himself to be kept here. Only chance in the moment would decide which action he took. *Eternal, let my sister not be stupid and test me.*

Usilea's golden eyes traveled from the blade of his knife to his face, and then behind him, presumably to where Renna stood. His sister's mouth worked, then she shook her head.

"So many times, I wanted to tell you. I wanted to tell you everything." Her voice trailed off to a whisper. "But our parents forbade it. They said that if I told you the truth, it would mean you would be surrendered to the Sanctuary. My silence protected you."

"And condemned so many others," Renna answered, her normally gentle voice shaking with anger. "But what care you for their sakes?"

Usilea scowled. "Silence, Mender. I'll not stand by and let you run away and take my only brother with you!"

Jaric glared at her. "We are bound together."

"Yes, I know you are. The soul-mingling." Bitterness—and perhaps a touch of envy—colored her voice. "I sensed it as soon as I saw you two together."

"What of it?" Renna's voice faltered slightly at the end.

"It is a special gift of Menders, as well as other gifted individuals. I have made some study of it. Your souls call to each other upon the emergence of your gifts and join during sleep. It is both mysterious and forbidden by the Sanctuary, for your souls might choose someone inappropriate." Her lips curved up slightly. "As your souls have already, despite the famed tonic given to Menders upon the start of their sixteenth year."

"So it was the tonic…" Renna's voice turned bitter. "Meant to enable healing and rest."

Usilea shook her head. "All of that was a lie to keep you within Sanctuary control. No one could know the truth about you."

Footsteps echoed behind him, and Renna's voice sounded closer to his ear. "Please, if you have any caring left within you, help us free my father. He is near death, but at least allow him to pass his final days in peace away from here."

His sister's face closed off. "I cannot allow that. You would expose too much, too soon."

"No!" Renna's despair tore at Jaric's heart. "I promise, I wouldn't—"

"Yes, you would. And I want you to, but not yet. Soon." Usilea's face softened to deep compassion and sorrow. "I have wept over this room since I first learned of its purpose, of which you only know a part. Which is why I cannot allow you to leave my country."

Jaric's jaw set. Now came the moment. The one he couldn't visualize, could not even consider in any part of his conscious mind.

Still, a moment that would have to come, if he and his beloved would be free.

And they would be free.

Usilea took one step toward him, then another, each as hesitant as the tremble of her lips, the fear in her eyes. For a moment, her youth lay evident on her face.

"But there is another way. A way that could help far more than you know." She focused on Renna. "It may even preserve the life of your father."

Renna gasped. "How?"

"Don't be fooled, Renna," Jaric cut in. "Lea has been trained by my parents in manipulation and has lied to me thus far."

"Lied to you badly. Do you not remember that as well?" Usilea took another step forward, her hands out, beseeching. "You have seen the cost upon me. You promised you would help me, that you would stand by me." She raised her head. "Help me now, and in turn, I can ensure you live together in as much peace as a sovereign can grant."

"A *future* sovereign." Jaric raised his eyebrows. "Yet not free?"

"We are none of us truly free, but each a slave to whatever we desire and pursue most," she answered.

"Writings from the old texts of the Eternal," Renna breathed.

Usilea nodded. "*The Way of Surrender*. It is one of the few things that has brought me peace in my life. And now I offer that to you. Lose that which you desire most to stand for the truth, and you might find it again."

"Might?"

"Nothing we devise is certain." She shrugged, coming to stand before him. Near enough for him to strike, yet she called for no guards, did nothing to protect herself. "Sometimes I find peace in that when I consider my arranged marriage—or grieve that my brother could leave me so easily."

Silence passed in pinprick moments, searing every part of Jaric's mind. For all that he could tell, Usilea seemed to be speaking plainly. But there was no surety of that, a fact the ribbons of tension over his heart made clear.

A hand squeezed his bicep. He glanced down into the endless depths of Renna's cobalt eyes, eyes that were filled with tears and a new resolve. A conviction he had never seen or felt in their midnight encounters, though it seemed familiar. It was borne out of the very words of strength he had spoken to her, encouraging her to stand up, to speak out.

To fight back in whatever way she was able. Even if it looked like giving up.

He could read the words on her face. *Often we must give up one thing to gain something far better.*

Is this truly better? Jaric knew he didn't need to say the words. Their souls were well acquainted with this discussion.

A discussion of pushing, of pulling, of waves crashing against immutable rock and shadows flowing around impenetrable darkness until finally, they both came to understanding.

To purpose. Together.

Though it cost them everything.

He turned back to Usilea.

"What is your plan?"

Her shoulders sagged in relief, then she straightened once more and raised her chin, every inch the crown princess. "Our parents have told me much, and I have discovered much more myself. They chose me as heir because I was not cursed as you were by their crimes, and because they thought to mold me. Those crimes, those heedless words they spoke, will be their undoing." Her eyes glittered with fierce strength, glazed with tears. "And there will be justice for all my people."

"Our people," Renna said, soft but firm.

Jaric set his jaw, hearing the vow in her voice. Agreeing with the barest incline of his head.

As long as Usilea's words proved as true now as they had been false earlier.

He might not be able to trust her.

But he could give her one more chance.

CHAPTER THIRTEEN

While Jaric and his sister differed in many ways—him tall, his eyes green, hers golden—in one aspect they were identical: their capacity to argue and stubbornly hold to their own views. No matter how late at night it was, or how much they had already debated matters.

Renna yawned. *Which has been quite a long time.*

At Renna's insistence, Usilea had directed the Attendants to properly dress Renna's father and take him to her private carriage, which was far more palatial than Anlyn's respectably ornate vehicle. Within the carriage had been space for Ertax to be stretched out on cushions on the floor, as well as room for Usilea and her guards to sit on one side with Jaric and Renna on the other. Keddyr and Anlyn had been ordered to return to her estate quietly, and had ignored the order equally as quietly. They now followed the royal carriage to the palace. Usilea had not said a word against their disobedience.

Then again, the princess and prince were much occupied with other matters. Once Usilea and Jaric had locked eyes in the carriage, they had commenced discussions and negotiations. At first, Renna had tried to keep up, casting in her ideas and opinions about the upcoming showdown with the king and queen.

A confrontation with the highest rulers in the land. Just the thought made her stomach twist and turn into knots, distancing her from the debate. Who was she to demand they change? How would such a scenario even take place?

Meanwhile, the siblings continued to argue.

"No matter what significant blackmail you have against our parents, what is to stop them from simply arresting or imprisoning us?" Jaric demanded.

A reasonable thought. Renna yawned again into her hand.

Usilea's eyes hardened. "They would not dare. While they may have purposefully chosen to belittle you, my brother, they have elevated me to a high and valued position. The royal guards, especially the ones who personally watch over our immediate family, will be torn in loyalties sufficiently for me to gain the upper hand."

The guards on either side of her remained stoic, their auras telling Renna about a sore muscle here, a throbbing temple there. Nothing about their loyalties.

Jaric scowled, stroking Renna's knee absently as his expression turned inward, assessing and considering other alternatives.

"And you refuse to share the substance of this blackmail with us?" Renna asked in the quiet moment.

"Are you sure you want to know?" Usilea's expression turned sympathetic, her gaze darting between Renna and her father.

"If I didn't, I wouldn't have asked."

"Then perhaps it is I who do not want to sully whatever shreds of good opinion you might yet hold of me." A shadow passed over her face. "As hard as it may be for you to believe, I am not your enemy. I would like to be your friend, even a sister, from what little I know of you."

A sister? Renna frowned. No one had ever owned her as such. There might have been a friend or two when she was younger, but pain and age had silenced those memories.

If we are to be family, then you shouldn't keep such a secret from me," she answered softly. "You and Jaric might be skilled at politics and wordplay, but I don't want either of them. I only want to see the right and just things done."

And then to be left alone. But the latter would not happen, it seemed.

The princess nodded. "Yes. That is a fair request." She turned to Jaric, but he only drilled her with an expectant stare. She rubbed the space between her eyebrows. "Very well. As you know, our line began with the Searlens taking over after the war and creating the Sanctuary in Syrus to protect Menders, the most valuable and sacrificial among us. The Mender Sanctuary was meant to be optional, as was the healing. No Mender was confined to the Sanctuary. It was only meant to be a place of refuge and respite from daily life. For aside from the gift of Receiving and the peculiar communion of soul-mingling, there is no difference in our kinds."

Renna nodded. Such things had been told to her by her parents.

"Go on, Lea." Jaric's words were clipped.

She winced at his tone. "Over the years, protectiveness became jealousy, which in turn became entitlement. Menders were rounded up and kept within the Sanctuary, ostensibly for their own good. They were no longer given the right to volunteer for or abstain from Mending. Healing at the Sanctuary was considered a royal right, not a free gift from a willing heart. Menders were seen as commodities to be used and disposed of, and they were cared for as tools, not as beings with souls. And as sovereigns grew used to living longer and longer, they became . . . discontent. They desired to extend their health evermore." Usilea paused, clutching at her skirt and eventually releasing the fabric in wrinkled bunches. "I believe it was our grandparents who began the ritual of Final Intake, on behalf of our father, the future king."

The name, spoken with revulsion by Usilea, was foreign to Renna. "What is this?"

"I promise you, I have never taken of a Mender." Her eyes pleaded with Renna. "The very idea is thoroughly repugnant."

Jaric leaned forward. "What is it, Lea?"

"When a Mender dies, what do you believe happens to their bodies?"

"They are destroyed in a fire," Renna answered. A disturbing ritual, when burial was the only way to set a soul at rest.

"They . . . are not." Usilea inhaled sharply, and her next words came out in a rush of agonized speech. "The bodies of Menders are thoroughly drained of blood, which is used in a variety of tonics, salves, and other items. Then the corpse is dried, the bones ground up for more potions and powders said to have healing properties, and every last part of the desiccated flesh and skin is likewise pulverized to be . . . ingredients."

Renna's mouth fell open. Somehow, she could find no strength to close it. All of her flagging energy was directed at trying to comprehend the princess's words. To burn the bodies was merely unorthodox. But this...

She stared at her father, his chest rising and falling in slow, uneven breaths. She was unable to imagine him being so horribly desecrated, used as just another object.

A tightness on her knee caught her attention. Jaric clutched her almost hard enough to cause pain. Renna placed her fingers over his hand, massaging gently. Not to offer comfort, but to commiserate. It was all she had left.

Jaric huffed out a long breath. "Usilea, for our parents, for our grandparents, to profane the bodies of others so, to profane themselves by ingesting the blood and marrow of another human..."

"I know. It violates our most sacred laws." She mirrored his horrified expression. "They did it at first to preserve the life of our father. Mender after Mender failed to fully heal him, but ingesting parts of Menders appeared to be more . . . effective. And by then, Menders were seen as tools to be used. It was only one more step. When he grew older, he didn't age. Our mother noticed this and, well..." Usilea's lips twisted. "Our parents love each other. Mother had stayed by his side during his illness. He didn't want her to suffer aging either. After she began the Final Intake, they started considering who among the Royal Cabinet might benefit in exchange for their loyalty to the throne."

Renna's stomach roiled as she fought the urge to gag. To burst into tears. To express in a thousand ways how heart-breakingly wrong this all was.

Usilea kept speaking. "I knew something must be done, especially when they began speaking of changing the laws so that the Final Intake wouldn't be illegal. They began to conceive plans on how to shift public opinion, little by little. I had to act. I prayed to the Eternal, I sought guidance from study, I considered strategy after strategy. Still, I was at a loss—and then you two met at the ball and created such a stir with your antics." Her expression softened with warmth and irritation. "It was difficult for me to placate our parents, and yet, I found hope in your union. Here were allies, at last."

A thread of guilt tightened Renna's chest. Not intensely, for she hadn't known of what Usilea revealed. She couldn't be blamed for what was kept from her.

And yet . . . she had not thought of others. Of what she and Jaric could do to change the kingdom through their union. She'd only thought of escape. Of freedom.

Her eyes met his, and she read the same regret there. Fierce anger as well, and profound irritation, but also the guilt of not questioning. Not even trying to remain.

At last, they broke their stare.

"We knew none of this," Jaric said simply.

"Now you do," Usilea replied. The carriage came to a stop. "Now you have no excuse. And your lives are at stake as well, for do not think my parents are blind to the threat your union holds. Corenne Valtor, quiet rebel of the Sanctuary. Jaricob Searlen, the outcast son who, it is believed, carries the gift of Mending as a consequence of their foul actions. Together, you are formidable—if you do not run away and hide all that you could offer."

"Which is?"

Usilea stared out the window at the palace walls, resplendent in yellows and reds and blues. "At my age, I am able to inherit the throne if my parents are found unfit or choose to willingly surrender their authority—as long as I have a responsible regent to assist me." She stared at Jaric, then continued. "This also gives me the weight of an entire kingdom to rule. The Mender Sanctuary is only a part of that kingdom. I have long thought Menders should be self-governed by those who understand the burden of Mending best."

A silence fell in the interior of the carriage. Of all the statements Usilea had made, this one stole the last of Renna's words, even within her thoughts.

So softly, she uttered, "You would have those of us who carry one burden take on another, even greater?"

"I ask no more than I must take on myself. At least, you, Renna who would be my sister, would not carry the burden alone."

The melancholy comfort in the princess's eyes undid Renna. How long had she desired companionship—not of many, but of a few who could speak and understand? How long had this young heir lived in the shadows, entrapped as Renna had been, albeit in a different state?

It was not right for either of them to live that way. Renna caught Jaric's eye. For any of them to be so abandoned and misused . . . but running away was not the answer, even if it beckoned to her soul.

Such reckless freedom always had a cost.

Slowly, she took Jaric's hand, felt his strength flow through her. A squeeze of his hand revealed his conviction. Renna reached out her other hand to Usilea. With a faint, growing smile, the princess took it.

"You do not stand alone," Renna said.

"Good." Usilea's eyes shone.

A loud knocking broke through the moment. The next instant, a bright light flashed, and a blast like thunder shook the carriage, nearly rocking it over. Fear shot through Renna, and she instinctively looked outside, dropping Jaric and Usilea's hands. Vestiges of smoke filtered through the air, revealing rows of marching soldiers, their swords drawn and expressions grim.

She turned to Jaric.

He looked out the window and cursed, then gestured to Usilea's guards. "Lea, are they loyal?"

"If we were not, your sister would have been imprisoned long ago," one said with a derisive look. "Your highnesses, Mendor Valtor, run! Run with those in the carriage behind us."

Yes, Keddyr and Anlyn. They would help.

"We'll offer what distraction we can." The guard's jowly face turned grim. "The guards outside aren't the only ones with fancy gunpowder tricks."

Usilea nodded. "Quickly! We must get to the court."

"The court?" Renna exclaimed. "But don't their majesties mean to kill us?"

"Officially, our parents can do no such thing," Jaric said. "The guards are to arrest us and bring us before the authorities, I'm certain." He grabbed the door handle. "But if we are killed during the attempt, it is considered a tragedy of our resistance, not murder."

"I truly hate our laws," Usilea growled.

"Agreed."

"What about my father?" Renna moved toward him protectively.

The second guard gave her a stern look. "If we cannot defend the least among us, then we are not worthy of being called guards of the royal family—which includes you now, I believe. And him." His square jaw tightened. "No harm will come to him."

"You give your word?"

"As much as I can with this uncertainty." The guard narrowed his eyes. "You must go now, my lady!"

The honorific felt odd and unnatural, enough to jolt her into action.

Jaric nodded to the guard who had first spoken. "Release your flashsparks."

The guard nodded, grabbing something from within his tunic.

Jaric flung open the door away from the encroaching forces and grabbed Renna's hand. She tensed and gripped Usilea's hand in hers.

As one they leaped from the carriage, just as the world exploded around them.

Chapter Fourteen

Jaric dropped into a crouch, fighting to keep his balance with the impact. Renna's hand escaped his as she immediately dropped and rolled out from the impact. A skill from an active childhood of somersaults and other vigorous play—he knew that from their soul-mingling.

A brief rush of attraction filtered through him. Again, she proved she was capable. Not that she should ever have to endure an attack again, but his beloved would not cow under pressure.

And neither of them would abandon this fight.

He grabbed Renna's arm and yanked her up, then sought about for Usilea. His sister struggled to her feet in a nearby shrubbery. He and Renna immediately ran to assist her, but Lady Anlyn reached the princess first.

"Come now, Your Majesty. First you dress like a peasant, then you dig around in the soil as well."

Usilea blinked and shook her head. "You're incorrect. It's 'Your Highness' for a princess."

"Don't fool yourself, my dear. You'll be a ruling monarch soon enough, after we face the court. Or why else are you bothering?"

Jaric stared at the noblewoman. "How did you know?"

"King Obrik and Queen Giala have made it clear in the court that they are very involved in overseeing the Menders. 'Our treasured heritage' so they say. It stands to reason they would have to be deposed in order to change how Menders are treated. I'm amenable to plant of action. The time has come."

"For what reason do *you* want to depose the king and queen?" he demanded.

She shrugged. "Maybe after years of acting the part of a widowed matchmaking coquette, I'm elevating my goals to a higher endeavor. After all, a woman needs a hobby besides searching for another husband—and I've found one, so the entire quest is nearing completion."

What in all stones? Jaric shot a glance at Keddyr.

His friend's face turned sheepish and yet defiant.

Another flashspark explosion filled the air with searing heat and acrid powder. Jaric set his jaw. Enough chatter. He could attempt to beat some sense into Keddyr afterward on the sparring field, although he had little hope his friend would listen. Stubbornness was a trait they shared in equal measure.

"Follow me. I know a side entrance."

Thank the Eternal he'd made it.

He grabbed Renna's hand and broke into a run, darting through a gap in the hedgerows. Usilea kept pace on his other side, with Keddyr and Lady Anlyn falling in behind them. Good. Keddyr could provide rearguard, and while Anlyn and Renna had little to no fight training, Usilea was far more equipped. Jaric had trained her.

"A side entrance?" Usilea gave him a sidelong glance as she

veered around a bed of foxflowers. "What side entrance do you speak of that our parents have not discovered?"

Jaric smirked. "One that I personally created in the spare time I had as an unwanted second son."

"Unwanted?" Her face fell, but no surprise showed on her features. Only regret, touched with guilt. "Brother, I assure you, I never thought such a thing."

"I know." He cut through another section of hedge, forcing his way through the brush. Behind him, Renna followed without issue—even with gusto—though her face was pinched with worry, doubtless about her father.

Jaric squeezed her hand. "We had no other choice."

"I know." She swiped at the wetness on her face with her free hand, her deep blue eyes turning stoic. "Whether he lives or dies is in the Eternal's care now. We must continue on."

"Yes." He fought the urge to take her in his arms, to press his face into her hair and offer the comfort she needed. But now was not the time. If they didn't make it to the court, they would all perish and whatever feelings he had would be irrelevant.

Another skidding turn around a corner, and they reached the hidden doorway. He pressed the proper sequence of stones, and a small partition slide aside. Usilea's mouth dropped open.

"You put all this effort into creating a way to leave the palace unnoticed?"

"A man has his priorities when he wants to elope with his beloved."

Renna gave a small startled squeak. He assumed of joy. She did have odd mannerisms.

Usilea huffed. "As your future sovereign, I am forbidding you from wasting this talent only on yourself."

He spared a moment to scowl back at her before continuing

forward. Steep steps led down to a passageway, dimly lit by mineral glow rods. Never bright enough for daily use, but enough to keep them from stumbling into walls. "As your older brother, I will be much surprised the day you succeed in ordering me about merely based on your whims."

Usilea frowned back at him. "What about the needs of your queen and people?"

"Are you preparing your grand edicts at this moment?" His hackles rose along with the hairs on the back of his neck. Was she going to attempt to assert rank now? Yes, they were on their way to depose their parents, and yes, Usilea was capable of leading, but that didn't mean she could command him hither and thither like an ordinary servant.

She grabbed his tunic and stared up at him. "No, but I need to know I can trust you beyond the moment, Jaric. You help me now, but what of tomorrow, or the next day?"

"Find me then and ask me," he said shortly. "I'll continue to be here because I choose to be."

"And what if you choose not to be?"

They had halted, not more than a half dozen steps from the end of the passageway. The walls closed around them, air still and stale, their backs stiff.

A throat cleared. Jaric turned to Renna.

"A passageway such as this would be ideal for Menders to use, to return to the Sanctuary at will," she said quietly, "instead of being locked away or hounded at the gates."

He studied her, something within him softening. "An excellent proposal, Renna."

Usilea also studied her thoughtfully. "Indeed."

"I do have those, on occasion." Renna gave a half-smile. "Another one is that we should continue on to the court, yes? Unless you want to remain here, in which I will then need to do quite a bit of redecorating—perhaps knock down a few walls—lest I go mad from the tight quarters."

She stared around ruefully, her sincere dislike apparent.

Something in the echoes of their souls resonated with her words, enough that Jaric gently touched her shoulder and continued on. Behind him, he could hear Usilea muttering something about being convinced he was in love because she had never seen anyone silence her brother so.

Yet that was the difference. Renna never sought to silence him or control him, never acted as though he were unwanted or even a threat. When their souls had first mingled, there had only been curiosity, wariness, and then relief—mirroring their later meeting in-person.

He reached the blank wall that signified the end of the passage and the exit on the other side. Jaric pressed his ear to the stone, trying to discern if there were any guards on the other side. His neck muscles tensed.

Footsteps echoed distantly on the stone. Only a few.
Nothing.
Jaric inhaled noiselessly, exhaling in the same manner.
Nothing.

At last, he touched Renna's shoulder again, leaning in to speak in her ear in a barely perceptible voice.

"As soon as I open, we run. Do you know where the Court Chamber is?"

She shook her head, a strand of her hair tickling his lips.

"Then take my hand, and don't let go."

She nodded.

Jaric gestured to Usilea, urging her closer, and spoke to her of the plan in the same nearly silent speech. She in turn passed the information to Anlyn and Keddyr, then stared at him intently.

All was ready.

One final pressing of his ear, one final check for guards.

His fingers found the edges of the exit, and he pressed in the key sections that would open the panel.

It slid aside into the grooves Jaric had cut into the wall. The other side remained shrouded in shadows, as befit a little-used portion of the palace that housed supplies for the servants.

One final breath.

They ran down the hallways of the palace, passed tapestries and a few bewildered servants awake at this late hour. Past guards who shouted at them to halt, to submit to arrest.

All to enter the Court Chamber.

Even as their shoes pounded the stone, a faint humor lightened his heart.

Only a night ago, he was escaping this wretched place. Now he was racing into the depths of it, right to the very two people who had sought to cast him aside.

His parents, who would this night be cast aside in turn, if Usilea's words were to be trusted. It seemed his sister had done more scheming and planning than he had ever given her credit for. Another unsettling thought he pushed aside, along with the nerves in his stomach.

There was only this moment. The sweat streaking his face, the rush of exertion, the feel of Renna's hand in his. The satisfaction of finally taking hold of his own fate, one way or another, instead of running from it or surrendering to the decisions of others.

No, the surrender was his own.

The small side door to the Court Chamber lay ahead, along with the usual outfit of guards. Warning flashed through him, and he skidded to a halt. Intimidating these guards with speed would serve no purpose, since only one person could fit through the doorway at a time.

Next to him, Renna clenched her shaking hands and lifted her chin in quiet defiance.

"Halt in the name of the king and queen!" intoned one of the guards, pointing the sharp metal end of his halberd at them.

The thud of heavy, armored footsteps echoed behind them. A quick glance revealed they were surrounded.

Another guard spoke up—this one seemed familiar. Had Jaric rushed past his ineffective blocking techniques the other night? "Prince Jaricob Searlen, you are under arrest for violating a most solemn vow to their majesties, and for desertion of the palace during the Royal Fellowship Ball."

Jaric sighed. "Who would have known they would be so affronted over the matter of announcing a bride?"

There was a slight hesitation on the part of the guard, along with a flash of confusion across his face. Nevertheless, he continued. "You are charged with consorting with a treasonous member of a heretofore unknown rebellious sect."

"Am I, now? Rather impressive of me, considering how they kept me caged quite competently. On what evidence do they base these accusations?"

"That is not our place to know. Come with us before the court and make your case there." The guards pressed closer. "The rest of you will likewise be escorted into the Court Chamber."

A gasp of protest issued from Renna, then was abruptly quieted at a touch from Usilea, her face set in a mask of determination.

Jaric understood. They had made it to the Court Chamber unscathed. Now that they were there, she was prepared for the rest. Eternal willing.

"Very well." He held up his hands. "I surrender."

Again. This was growing tiresome.

Yet it was the only way.

One by one, they were led through the side entrance and across the massive circular floor inlaid with the Edrin crest of a sapphire falcon clutching a golden sword. Around them were arranged polished tables which held the members of the court—seventeen in total, fifteen now as Anlyn and Keddyr were in the center area. Jaric's gaze skimmed over the figures, and he turned to face his parents on the dais that loomed over him. Queen Giala was mockingly triumphant, King Obrik more stern than usual. Their usual expressions, chosen specifically to contrast with each other.

"And so, our wayward son returns to us," Queen Giala proclaimed. "Although with no suitable bride."

Jaric smiled thinly. "Ah, but I have made my choice of wife. I was merely delayed from declaring her by other matters."

"Yes, the rebel girl, Corenne M'Valo," she commented, glaring at Renna.

"She is a Mender—"

"She is the daughter of rebels. Ertax and Nephyna Valtor disobeyed our laws and kept themselves from the Sanctuary we so graciously provided for their safety and security."

"Indeed," King Obrik rumbled.

Renna inhaled quickly and spoke up. "My parents were peaceful. My father only wished to serve as priest in our northern village. They surrendered themselves to the Attendants when visited upon. My family has served faithfully in the Sanctuary."

"Until now," Queen Giala shot back. "Until the night you escaped with the express intent to seduce and corrupt the Prince of Searlen, denying your duties as a Mender."

"Furthermore, you sought to deprive your father of his final rites within the Mender Sanctuary."

Renna's olive face paled. "Who told you that?"

King Obrik stared over her head. Right at Usilea.

Jaric's stomach sank.

"Her Highness, the Crown Princess Usilea Searlen. As always, a most devoted servant of the throne."

Anger flowed through Jaric. He scowled at his sister, who only returned his glare with a mildly apologetic expression.

"My apologies, dear brother. But I owe my final allegiance to the welfare of my kingdom, not your trivial dalliances. Such as they are." She gave him a dismissive glance, as though he were known for courtly intrigues instead of ignoring them like an annoying insect.

His sister. The real traitor among them.

She turned to face the rest of the court in a sweeping action. "And it is out of that profound loyalty that I must bring a far more heinous crime to the court."

The king and queen stilled. Usilea gave them a small smile. "It, too, involves Corenne M'Valo's father."

His parents relaxed.

"Go on, my daughter," Queen Giala said, returning the smile.

"I have discovered the traitorous Mender's reasons for escaping with her father—the belief that the final rites for Menders would somehow bring him harm. She believed that the Sanctuary defiled the blood and bones of dying Menders."

Jaric narrowed his eyes. Renna had known nothing of the desecration until Usilea had told her. What was his sister doing?

King Obrik leaned forward in his throne. "What is your meaning, Crown Princess Usilea?"

The use of her full name was a subtle warning.

She only exhaled a sound of deep sadness. "As a devoted servant of Edrin, I took it upon myself to investigate the matter and bring it before the court. And I have learned these beliefs are entirely..." Usilea paused. "Entirely true."

Upset murmurs filled the court. Before them, Queen Giala rose from her throne. "What you speak is impossible! The care and protection of Menders is personally overseen by the reigning monarchs as our duty."

"A duty you have abused for your own benefit. My lords and ladies, have you never wondered how your sovereigns appear so well-preserved? For even into their sixth decades, they appear no more than thirty years apiece." The murmurs among the court increased in volume. Usilea continued. "It is result of potions made from Mender blood, salves of Mender bones, treatments of jellied Mender tendons and marrow. They ingest the life of their people for their own gain!"

King Obrik's expression twisted with rage.

"You forget your place, daughter, with these grievous lies!"

"Yes, lies and falsehoods!" Queen Giala declared.

Usilea stared back at the king, then abruptly turned to Anlyn. "Tell me, Lady Anlyn, what is a consequence of defiling Mender bodies by ingesting their parts? For we tried someone in such a case years ago, and you were part of that tribunal, as I remember."

"Indeed, I was." The noblewoman's eyes glinted. "The children of those engaging in such an act could carry the Mender gift. That which is thought to only come from the union of two Menders could come from the union of two defilers."

"Is this agreed and accepted by the court to be standard knowledge, given that the Lady Anlyn was so involved in this trial?"

Heads nodded around the court tables.

"Then there is only to prove the matter—"

"Ungrateful, treacherous urchin!" Queen Giala spat. "You may have betrayed our confidence, but you will not dishonor our name, nor our love!" Her face flushed dark as she turned to Jaric. "Not if I take yours in return, son."

She made a flicking gesture with her fingers. Something sharp and silvery flew at Renna.

"No!" The words gargled in Jaric's mouth.

He leaped in front of her.

A sharp, piercing pain sliced through his gut.

Renna's mouth opened in a wordless scream as he sank to his knees, clutching at the blade. Blood spurted between his fingers as he fell to his side.

Around him, so distantly, he heard shouts, shrieks. Demands for explanations, for justice.

Waves of agony rolled through him.

"Jaric? Jaric, no. No! Not for me."

Renna's face was pinched with worry and wet with tears. Her hands pressed over his, trying to stop the flow of blood.

"Always . . . for you." He gritted his teeth. "Can't . . . let them . . . win."

"You can't die! That would let them win!" Her voice choked with sobs. "I can't heal you, my love."

"Jaric, it wasn't supposed to end this way," Usilea said on his other side, cradling his face, her eyes disbelieving. Anguished.

"Tell that . . . to our parents."

"No," she whispered. "Not after all these years. Not when I can finally speak truly with you again."

She tilted her forehead to touch his.

Lightning flickered through him at the contact. Brilliance flashed before his eyes. All his agony seemed to pulse at that singular point. Excruciating, like a nail being pounded from within his head outward.

Then blessed relief. Every twinge of pain, every wrenching twist of his stomach, gone.

It was all gone.

There was a fresh scream. "The princess!"

He jumped to his feet, suddenly filled with energy. His mind was still spinning, trying to comprehend.

Usilea lay on the ground, a dark stain trickling from her stomach, her eyes shut with pain. Alarm shot through him. He reached for her—but Renna held up a hand, her expression bewildered.

"Your injury . . . passed from you . . . to her." She breathed. "Impossible."

"Is she—?"

"Already, she begins to heal from your wounds."

Usilea Received from a Mender.

He swallowed. "How? She never—"

"Sometimes the power doesn't fully manifest until age sixteen."

"She just turned. But no one can heal a Mender."

"My father once said the Eternal does as he chooses. Your parents' actions were bound to have odd effects." Renna shook her head, just as confused as he was, yet so very joyful beneath her worry for Usilea.

A hand pressed into his shoulder. Jaric glanced up at Keddyr, his eyes taking in the scene. He raised his eyebrows.

Announce this to the room? He nodded, muttering, "Keep it simple."

No need to explain the additional surprises in Usilea's ability.

Keddyr cleared his throat. "The crown princess Receives the deadly injury from her brother. She is a Mender! This is your proof! Their majesties have ingested—have defiled—the bodies of those who were living. A horrific crime!"

At that, the court filled with a fresh uproar. Accusations flew right and left, along with questions and sharp retorts.

Jaric glanced at the dais. Guards surrounded the king and queen, halberds out.

One word filtered from the throng.

Dethrone. Dethrone.

Dethrone.

CHAPTER FIFTEEN

She had endured the death of her mother, coerced servitude, and assisted in the deposing of the ruling monarchs.

Yet nothing had prepared Renna for the road that now lay before her with glimmering golden stones rimming the edges. Crushed stones of deep sapphire filled the pathway, which began at the end of the long drive at the front of the palace and ended inside the main ballroom. Crowds of people stood on either side in their finest clothing, whatever that entailed for a noble, merchant, or peasant, as all had been invited.

Eternal help her, it seemed as though half the kingdom had come.

She ducked back into the silvery-gray tent, her chest rising and falling rapidly. Each breath ached, despite the tailored fit of the deep emerald gown that flowed over her body into a mercifully short train. Despite weeks of effort, Renna had not mastered a full train, and Usilea said it was better to be a little nontraditional than to trip down the aisle.

None of which would matter if she never made it down the aisle. A highly likely prospect, considering how her heart pounded in her ears.

Why did I have to fall in love with a prince?

She sat in a chair near the entrance, shoving her face into the bouquet of mist orchids. Inhaling. Exhaling. The fresh, salty scent of the deep violet flowers did nothing to calm her mood.

Renna, you can do this.

Yes, she could be married. She wanted more than anything to be married to Jaric.

But this wedding was another matter entirely.

A hand settled on her shoulder, and a sleeve gently sloped down her arm.

"To think that I would live to see you in a green gown," a gentle male voice intoned. "I only wish your mother were here."

A smile twitched her lips. "Me, too. Although she might be ashamed of how scared I am. You were both always far braver. You turned yourselves in to the Attendants fearlessly, while I cried."

"You were a sheltered child." A square, solid hand similar to her own tilted her chin up. "No longer a child, my daughter, yet you are still unaware of much of the world. Receive the Eternal's grace."

She stared into Ertax Valtor's olive face, still far thinner and more wrinkled than it should be, but real and there in front of her. All courtesy of Usilea's rare and inexplicable gift to Receive from Menders. She couldn't restore the life force he had expended, so now he resembled one of seventy years rather than forty. But he was alive, far healthier than before, and here to see her wedding day.

A wedding she would soon ruin by cowardice.

Renna's stomach clenched. "I'm sorry. It's just so very long, and—and shouldn't you be at the end, Father?"

After all, he was the priest officiating the ceremony, a position she had negotiated to honor her family and restore their good name. Usilea had readily agreed to this. After all, Ertax Valtor was now the senior priest of the royal temple as well as Renna's partner in managing the Mender Sanctuary.

Everything had fallen into place easily enough. All Renna had to do was walk down the aisle and marry Prince Jaric, regent to the new queen, with everyone staring at her and cheering—hopefully cheering, not slandering. Yet even if they weren't pleased, it wasn't personal. None of them knew her beyond a few public appearances she and Jaric had made in the two months after the dethroning of the old monarchs.

There would be noise, nonetheless. The ceremony was loud, wreathed in tradition and pomp, separate from her own preferences and choices. She stared at the bouquet. At least her favorite flowers were permitted.

The seat next to her creaked as her father sat down in it. "You are my daughter. I am here for you." He gave a crooked smile, his blue eyes twinkling. "And if you don't want to go down that aisle, there is little need for my duties. Although I did leave behind a prince who, beneath his stoicism, seemed equally uneasy about the fuss. I believe seeing and marrying you are the only reasons he remains."

"Well, there is the matter of our promises to Queen Usilea for a public ceremony of state used to foster the goodwill and merriment of the people." She tried to picture Jaric clad in deep emerald. Shades of green, symbolizing the new life of a newly married couple. His muscled build would likely strain at the fit, but his forest eyes would be even more striking.

It should be enough.

Why wasn't it?

She loved Jaric. Her soul longed for his and sought him every night.

Soon they would be the Duke and Duchess of Motarn, splitting their time between guiding the northeast dukedom and staying in Syrus where Jaric could assist Usilea and Renna could monitor the Sanctuary. Forever tied to responsibilities, service, and the welfare of the people.

"Have I told you how proud I am of you?" Her father gently stroked her back. "Your mother and I hoped the Eternal would use you to change the fate of Menders."

Renna frowned skeptically. "You said you surrendered because it was not your place to question the will of the Eternal, and he had willed our captivity. You warned against my resistance. You said that justice didn't matter."

"No, I said that justice comes with a price." He sighed. "I warned against your carelessness, against you making choices that only benefited us and came out of your own hurt. But your resistance against evil, your alliance with the prince your soul chose—those are gifts beyond my wildest expectations. You have restored justice."

"Now I will ruin it with my clumsiness and inexperience. Who am I to lead, to guide a people? I can't even walk down an aisle and face them!"

"You rode down it before for my sake, and now you walk to your prince." His expression turned stern, as it had in the past when she'd protested the difficulty of a particular climb up a mountain or dealt with the censure of a village child. "Corenne Valtor, you are compassionate, perceptive, and able to create beauty. You also have wise advisors and a clever husband who see your worth. Cease this protesting and take one step down the aisle to the future laid before you."

His kind but firm words cut through the spiral in her mind, anchoring her in the truth of the moment. Despite herself, she stood and smoothed down her dress with her gloved hands.

One final look through the opening to the aisle. "Only one step, yes?"

"One step." He nudged her forward. "And then one more. And one more. Until you can see the prince. Trust that he is waiting there. Trust that you will face your joys and difficulties together."

She inhaled, more slowly this time, then exhaled, breathing out fear and worry, enough that peace could overcome the small remainders.

I can do this.

"Very well," Renna nodded. "One step."

She managed to exit the tent. Uncertain crowds stared at her, then began cheering as festival bells and chimes rang out.

Her lips threatened to droop. She fought the urge and forced them to tilt upward, even as she raised her chin.

She could do one more step. Another.

A third, in the lightest of slippers that, astonishingly, did not cramp her feet. The royal cobbler had worked specifically for her comfort, and he had been surprisingly sympathetic to her dislike for shoes. There had been no disdain or dismissal.

Another step. Another.

Halfway down the aisle.

She knew that Usilea would also be waiting for her at the end of the aisle, overseeing the court aspects of the ceremony even as Ertax performed the religious rites. The young queen had become a fast friend over their shared preparations and understanding the loss of a mother. Lea's situation was even more trying, for her parents were imprisoned and sequestered far from the capital of Syrus.

In the wake of their mutual losses, Usilea and Renna were quickly becoming sisters.

Her smile grew. She'd never had a sister.

More steps. The grand doorway to the ballroom rose above her, festooned with more mist orchids and tallowfeather fronds. She walked beneath the greenery, keeping her gaze fixed ahead of her.

Her heart leaped.

Jaric stood on the first steps of the raised ceremonial platform. At his feet, Opal sat composed, although the labordrim wagged her tail violently upon seeing Renna. Renna smiled. She and the dog had become good friends, especially after Opal discovered how much Renna enjoyed long walks.

Next to Jaric stood her father, and a few steps above him, Usilea presided over the affair from her throne. Peevish worry briefly wrinkled Jaric's eyes, but every last one smoothed as he saw her. A look of profound awe overtook his handsome features. Warmth flooded her as their souls once more knew each other as truly theirs. A knowing that would only increase after their wedding, when the last barrier to their physical union fell away.

"Ahem." How the voice managed to interrupt her thoughts, Renna did not know. But she spared Anlyn a brief glance from where she stood at the very edge of the aisle. The noblewoman winked and whispered, "A room has been arranged for you both to, ahem . . . assist each other in changing from your wedding garments to your reception attire."

Now the warmth changed to a deep flush of embarrassment and relief—a relief that led to more embarrassment. Renna gave her the slightest head incline.

"Thank you," she murmured.

"You are very welcome. Don't break anything!"

The last part was certainly not in the quietest of whispers. Anlyn stepped back into the crowd next to Keddyr. A few patters of laughter floated through the crowd.

Renna found the last few steps remarkably easy to take. Away from Anlyn's remarks and toward her beloved, who gave her a curious look. She smiled at him in return, allowing herself another view of his form, head to toe. The emerald clothing suited his broad shoulders, strong arms, and muscled body better than she could have hoped.

Heat that had nothing to do with embarrassment swept through her.

Anlyn might have the subtlety of a mountain avalanche, but her procurement of the private room was certainly . . . thoughtful. Yes. Very thoughtful.

But first, there were the ceremony vows.

She ascended the final step to stand across from Jaric, setting her bouquet aside on a small table and picking up a golden gemstone, precious lightpur. The only gemstone appropriate for weddings, for with it they would mark the back of each other's hands and seal the marking with clear skinsenna.

"Now, let the wedding of Mender Corenne Valtor and Prince Jaricob Searlen the Tenth begin," Usilea's voice echoed through the chambers.

Soon, her words of royal institution were woven with Ertax Valtor's words of sacred duty. Of commitment and honor. Of placing the other before self. Of the beauty of love, stronger than stone.

With every word, with every declaration from her lips or from Jaric's, with the binding marks they made upon their hands, Renna knew the truth in her soul.

She was finally free.

Met By Midnight

Defiance is a whisper

In the darkening twilight before an undeserved death

Defiance is the clasp of hands

Before the final sacrifice

Defiance is the tear

On the cheek of a grieving daughter

Defiance is the choice

Of a dangerous mission into the unknown

Defiance is the surrender of will

Through an unlikely alliance

Met by midnight

For the greater good of a handful

Defiance is a whisper

Of love to the least

And this

And this

This is

Defiance

Hey there! Thanks so much for reading.

I wrote this book to be a light and hope in dark and difficult places. Sometimes growing up isn't easy, and we have to deal with hard things that aren't fair or right. But there is always hope.

Reviews are always appreciated!

For Usilea's story (yes, of course I had to write hers!) check out *Thorns At Sunrise*, the second book in the Star-Crossed Fairy Tale series. Her story is a retelling of Sleeping Beauty with a twist: the prince is the one who is asleep! Naturally, I had to do this, because Usilea is the one with a healing gift. But the prince definitely has things to say as well!

If you want to read more poetry,
check out my Unique Words poetry collections.

And for more exciting story news first,
sign up for my email newsletter, Bookish Vibes.

Have a wonderful day!

Acknowledgements

First and always, deepest thanks to my God and King. Writing with you is glorious.

Also, much gratitude to Stephen Ippolito, my fantastic husband who gives me many, many hugs.

Much thanks to alpha readers Sarah Delena White, Bethany A. Jennings, and Hannah Wilson for continuing to support this little book's journey—even when it meant I had to put off other stories you're waiting on. Y'all are awesome.

Huge appreciation to beta readers Kelly Thomas, H. L. Burke, Ggprof, and Brittany Gnizak. Your feedback was invaluable, and your excitement kept me going.

All the thanks to editor Sarah McConahy, who faithfully labored through some of the densest paragraphs I've ever written. Good job!

Loads of gratitude to Yvonne Less of Art 4 Artists for the perfect cover!

And finally, much appreciation to my faithful readers in both my reader group and scattered far and wide. Y'all are awesome, and I hope this encourages you.

ABOUT THE AUTHOR

Janeen Ippolito believes that books change the world. She's the multi-published author of 20+ books, including bestselling fiction, nonfiction, and poetry. She's also an experienced editor and marketing strategist, and for seven years was the CEO of Uncommon Universes Press, a publishing company with award-winning books. Oh, and she hosts the Author Elevate Podcast, a book business and marketing podcast, and speaks regularly at conferences. In her spare time, she helps her epic husband with his youth swordfighting ministry, indulges her foodie ambitions, reads whatever she wants, and explores a slew of random hobbies. Her life goals include traveling to Antarctica and riding a camel while wearing a party hat. She loves to collaborate and encourage, so connect with her on social media or at janeenippolito.com